How to Free a Naked Man from a Rock

How to Free a Naked Man from a Rock

AN ANTHOLOGY

edited by

Robert Kane
Stephanie Halpern
&
Spencer Seward

Red Hen Press | Pasadena, CA

How to Free a Naked Man from a Rock

Copyright © 2011 Red Hen Press

Introduction © 2011 Robert Kane

All rights reserved.

No portion of this work may be reproduced or transmitted in any form or by any means, electronic or mechanical, including photocopying and recording, or by any information storage or retrieval system, without permission in writing from Red Hen Press.

Book layout by Spencer Seward

Additional copy editing by William Goldstein and Chris Konish

ISBN: 978-1-59709-423-8

The City of Los Angeles Department of Cultural Affairs, Los Angeles County Arts Commission, National Endowment for the Arts, Kinder Morgan Foundation, Dwight Stuart Youth Fund, Ahmanson Foundation, the Brabson Library and Educational Foundation, the Meta and George Rosenberg Foundation, and the Transformation Trust partially support Red Hen Press.

First Edition
www.redhen.org

Acknowledgments

"The Matriot" by Frances Payne Adler. Published in *The Making of a Matriot* © Red Hen Press, 2003. Reprinted by permission of the author.

"Allegheny Love Letter" by Erinn Batykefer. Published in *Allegheny, Monongahela* © Red Hen Press, 2009. Reprinted by permission of the author.

"Pilgrimage Midsummer" by Elizabeth Bradfield. Published in *Interpretive Work* © Red Hen Press/Arktoi Books, 2008. Reprinted by permission of the author.

"Buffalo Dreams" by Bart Edelman. Published in *The Last Mojito* © Red Hen Press, 2005. Reprinted by permission of the author.

"The Bath" by Gaylord Brewer. Published in *Exit Pursued by a Bear* © Cherry Grove Collections, 2004. Reprinted by permission of the author.

"Faith" by Ed Falco. Published in *Mississippi Review* © Mississippi Review, 2006. Reprinted by permission of the author.

"Jazz is Not Enough" by Kate Gale. Published in *Selling the Hammock* © Red Hen Press, 1998. Reprinted by permission of the author.

"Odd" by DeWitt Henry. Published in *Safe Suicide* © Red Hen Press, 2008. Reprinted by permission of the author.

"The Orange Alert" by Douglas Kearney. Published in *Fear, Some* © Red Hen Press, 2006. Reprinted by permission of the author.

"Cinderella's Diary" by Ron Koertge. Published in *Fever* © Red Hen Press, 2006. Reprinted by permission of the author.

"Ballet Ghost" by Lisa C. Krueger. Published in *animals the size of dreams* © Red Hen Press, 2009. Reprinted by permission of the author.

"English Fundamentals" by Sebastian Matthews. Published in *The Chattahoochee Review* © The Chattahoochee Review, 2008. Reprinted by permission of the author.

"Something in the Belly" by Deena Metzger. Published in *Ruin and Beauty* © Red Hen Press, 2009. Reprinted by permission of the author.

"Real Estate" by Cecile Rossant. Published in *About Face* © Red Hen Press, 2004. Reprinted by permission of the author.

"Take a Left At My Mailbox" by Miriam Sagan. Published in *Map of the Lost* © University of New Mexico Press, 2008. Reprinted by permission of the author.

"Wondering Where the Whales Are" by Eva Saulitis. Published in *Leaving Resurrection* © Red

Hen Press, 2008. Reprinted by permission of the author.

"Five More Minutes" by Steven Schutzman. Published in *Eclectica Magazine* © Eclectica Magazine, October/November 2008. Reprinted by permission of the author.

"The Problem with Eating Japanese" by Julie Shigekuni. Excerpted from *Unending Nora* © Red Hen Press, 2008. Reprinted by permission of the author.

"In Praise, Ephemera" by Peggy Shumaker. Published in *Gnawed Bones* © Red Hen Press, 2010. Reprinted by permission of the author.

"Black Widow" by Maurya Simon. Published in *Cartographies* © Red Hen Press, 2008. Reprinted by permission of the author.

"Hallowe'en" by Lisa Russ Spaar. Published in *Glass Town* © Red Hen Press, 1999. Reprinted by permission of the author.

"The Death of Santa Claus" from *Shadow Ball: New and Selected Poems*, by Charles Harper Webb, © 2009. Reprinted by permission of the University of Pittsburgh Press.

"My Brother at the Canadian Border" by Sholeh Wolpé. Published in *The Scar Saloon* © Red Hen Press, 2004. Reprinted by permission of the author.

"The Deep Dive" by Sholeh Wolpé. Published in *Rooftops of Tehran* © Red Hen Press, 2008. Reprinted by permission of the author.

Contents

Introduction   9

Sebastian Matthews
   English Fundamentals   13
Charles Hood
   Where The Gangs Went   16
Frances Payne Adler
   The Matriot   20
Charles Harper Webb
   The Death of Santa Claus   23
Bart Edelman
   Buffalo Dreams   26
Sholeh Wolpé
   My Brother at the Canadian Border   30
Deena Metzger
   Something in the Belly   33
Lisa Russ Spaar
   Hallowe'en   38
Greg Sanders
   My Virtual Window   40
Erinn Batykefer
   Allegheny Love Letter   44
Cecile Rossant
   Real Estate   47
Ron Koertge
   Cinderella's Diary   50
DeWitt Henry
   Odd   52
Douglas Kearney
   The Orange Alert   58
Julie Shigekuni
   The Problem with Eating Japanese   61

LISA C. KRUEGER
   Ballet Ghost   66

SHELLEY SAVREN
   Yom Kippur   68

KATE GALE
   Jazz is Not Enough   72

GAYLORD BREWER
   The Bath   75

SHOLEH WOLPÉ
   The Deep Dive   78

ELIZABETH BRADFIELD
   Pilgrimage Midsummer   81

ED FALCO
   Faith   84

EVA SAULITIS
   Wondering Where the Whales Are   86

MAURYA SIMON
   Black Widow   104

MIRIAM SAGAN
   Take a Left At My Mailbox   106

PEGGY SHUMAKER
   In Praise, Ephemera   109

STEVEN SCHUTZMAN
   Five More Minutes   112

REX WILDER
   Three Boomerangs   137

Contributors' Notes   139

Dead Men Talking   151

Introduction

There's a 17-foot-tall naked guy who lives in Florence, Italy. He spends most of his time being ogled by anyone who cares to look. He's okay with this—he isn't the least bit ashamed. He's been doing this for over five hundred years, after all.

Come to think of it, maybe you've seen him before. His name is David. His picture's on the cover of this book.

David began his life as a very large, very lonely, and very slightly mistreated block of rock. When David's father, the legendary sculptor and all-around artistic genius Michelangelo, looked at that rock, however, he didn't just see a simple piece of weathered marble—he saw the stone boy, the statue, trapped inside.

When you look at rocks, what do you see inside? What are the things you see in *life* that no one else sees?

Chances are that you see some pretty cool, pretty wild stuff.

Michelangelo thought that David was pretty cool and wild, too, standing contraposto-style inside of that rock, staring out with those imposing eyes, and flexing those giant-slaying muscles. The problem was that, as long as David was trapped in the stone, no one but Michelangelo could see him! The solution? Michelangelo carved away at the rock until David was revealed.

The result? Now *everybody* can marvel over David. Michelangelo was right—the guy's pretty cool, even if he's too big to find a decent pair of jeans.

Take a look at the works of art the following authors freed from their minds. The process didn't work much differently for them than it did for Michelangelo—they saw the world in ways that no one else did, and they worked to free the visions in their minds so that *everyone* could see them.

Those same authors even wrote down some thoughts on *how* they freed the thoughts from their heads . . . and how they think that you could do the same. Maybe they're right, and maybe they're wrong. If they're right, let their words inspire you. If they're wrong, prove it by doing something better!

Okay, it's your turn to give it a shot. Take the sweetness, the sadness, the rage, the romance, the pathos, and the passion in your life. Look hard at them. No one else sees them the way that you do.

. . . Not *yet*.

I saw the angel in the marble and carved until I set him free.

—Sounds like something Michelangelo
probably would have said

Sebastian Matthews

English Fundamentals

When the man says he is going to read
the class a poem a friend has sent him—he wants

them to listen, to say what they think because
he has to tell his friend what he thinks—they stare

and laugh. "What are we going to say about it?
I mean what the heck do we know about poetry?"

The woman who says this, mother of two, deep
in her twenties but with a face closer to 40,

a husband in jail for slamming her against walls.
The others look at their hands or sit back

in their chairs and peer out the window.
When the poet's done reading the poem,

the class is sitting up, attention focused
on their teacher. "I understand that poem,"

the woman says, excited. "First there's the father,
then the fear, then the connection to the dog."

One young man, who has not spoken all semester,
looks up from his cuffs. "How does rain fall

in 'rotten' curtains?" "Ragged," someone offers.
"Oh." He looks back out the window.

The class discusses how rain does and
does not fall. The young man turns back,
agreeing that, indeed, rain could fall hard,
just he's never seen it like that where he's from.

   for Curtis Bauer

The Author Speaks!

A poet friend sent me an email about a class in which he was teaching one of my poems. I had written about taking a walk with my dog and missing my father, who had died a few years before. Inspired, I typed out the first few lines from his email. When I got to the woman raising her hand to ask a question, I began to imagine her life—and inner lives. Suddenly there was a quiet, possibly sullen student in the back. I kept imagining myself in front of that class, as if I was the teacher and it was my friend's poem we were discussing.

Take a snippet from an email or text message or some other found source and keep going with it, imagining a scenario, etc. Don't let yourself get trapped in your original, "triggering" subject. Allow yourself the freedom and room to follow the poem's "story" as it comes to you.

Questions:
1. What's happening at beginning of poem? Who is the "he"?
2. Talk about the characters in the poem. Do they seem realistic? Are they more like you than different from you?
3. Another poem is mentioned. Do you miss not seeing it? Why do you think the woman connects with it?
4. What do the last lines make you think of or feel? Why does the poet end the poem this way?
5. Why might the poem be titled "English Fundamentals"?

Charles Hood

Where The Gangs Went

After the earthquake it was different.
Zebras grazed the hillsides by the zoo,
would not go back in their pens. MTV
went off the air and nobody noticed.
Wild avocado trees grew up, fully formed,
around MacArthur Park Lake, so many
that even L.A. Cathedral became known
for its guacamole. Koreatown's menudo
was better than Glendale's. Two days
after Christmas there was a cold snap, even
the Los Angeles River froze solid—one morning
even the mayor was seen ice skating to work,
stopping here and there at the bonfires
of the homeless people to share hot cocoa
and hand around oranges he had bought
from the guy by the freeway. In Compton
it wasn't cold but hot like Hawaii, orchids
growing like weeds along all the cracks
and fences. You could tell Ghost Street Crips
from Hoover Crips by the new kind of orchid
(blue as coral lagoons) they wore in their hair.
All of the Bounty Hunters began singing
church music one morning, couldn't stop,
driving around with the windows down,
singing like choir boys, harmonizing
better than the 10 Line Crips, who were
more about spontaneous krump dancing.

In Venice the Sons of Samoa surfed
like 14 year old white kids, catching
crazy backside air and inventing a new kind
of board wax made from honeysuckle
and fossil tree amber. Peacocks
were taken on rides by fire trucks.
Cops taught the nuns magic tricks
and wore white gloves and top hats
even off duty. Officers from Hollenbeck
played soccer against the Tijuana Locos
and won. Pacoima Piru opened a farm
for horses too old to run at Santa Anita,
gave rides to kids, started breeding swans
so that abuelas having picnics at Hansen Dam
would have something to feed bits of bread.
Most people went to work by hot air balloon
but some rode horses, some rode in the wagon
towed by elephants just because they liked
waving to the jugglers and in-line skaters.
They knew that parrots had not always been
more common than pigeons, or they were not sure,
it became sort of hazy—what had it been like
before? Maybe there always had been waterfalls
splashing down the hillsides by Dodger Stadium,
grottos of ferns in bank lobbies, 400 flamingos
lined up like pink stilts along Compton Creek.
Was there a time cars did not come with free pianos?

You could tell the middle schools from the high schools
because each used a different kind of fireworks
at the end of the day, with triple sets on Fridays.
It must always have been like this, people said,
—*how could it ever have been any different*?
And they laughed, assuring themselves
that memories of the other life could not be true,
were just ghost stories to frighten the children,
touching one another on the shoulder
and smiling like the doors of cages left open so long
nothing will ever close them again.

The Author Speaks!

This poem takes place in an imaginary future and uses a kind of literary tradition from South America known as "magical realism." This is not science fiction exactly, but instead a technique allowing an author to relax the laws of probability—one gets to allow the world on the page to be as mysterious and exciting and dream-like as real life itself often is. It is not just that "truth is stranger than fiction," it is that fiction gets to be stranger than fiction, and it can be great fun to rewrite the laws of physics. This poem also wants to give you permission to defy the bad things in your life. If we want a different world, the first step is to dream it—and then to share that dream by writing it down. This is my "better world." What is yours?

Frances Payne Adler

The Matriot

During the Gulf War in 1991, I was sitting at my desk and heard on the radio that our defense forces had invented a missile and named it the "patriot." That evening, I invented a word, asking myself, what does a "matriot" look like?

> **Matriot** (ma' – tri – at) *noun* 1. One who loves his or her country. 2. One who loves and protects the people of his or her country. 3. One who perceives national defense as health, education, and shelter for all people in his or her country, and the world. (© FPA 1991)

Helen Vandevere, born 1904

There's not much that's important at my age
except making the world a better place.
What would *I* do?
I say we darn well better
get out on the streets again.
Everyone has to put their hand to the wheel
and get out and get off their butt
like in the sixties. We had compassion then,
and we've lost it. It breaks my heart.
I've lived through two depressions,
two of them. Everyone at that time
was just sick about the way things were,
just like now, only it's worse now.

I see things falling apart—
People, living on the streets.
Children, beaten in their homes.
Sick people without health care.
Imagine this, in a country
that spends so much on the war machine.
I'd spend the money on health instead.
I'd see that children are born healthy
and make sure they stayed that way.
All children no matter what age.
I'd clean the air, the water. I'd take away
all that polluting stuff they put on vegetables.
I'd promote the use of sun, sea, and wind
for natural energy. I'd save the forests,
especially the redwoods. I'd ban firearms.
I'd take away every nuclear device man to man.
No more wars, ever. *Now* we're talking health.
How are we going to pay for all this?
No one ever says we don't have enough
money to go to war. No one ever says
we don't have money for national defense.
This is national defense.

The Author Speaks!

The "Matriot" poem grew out of a moment of realization about the violence behind the word "patriot." During the Gulf War in 1991, I was sitting at my desk and heard on the radio that our defense forces had invented a missile and named it the "Patriot."

I was startled into consciousness. The word "patriot" comes from the Latin word, *pater*, meaning father. To me, "father" is an affectionate term, and I realized that, in naming a missile a "patriot," the role of the father was being maligned, and also that violence was being made synonymous with this role.

The "Matriot" poem was my way of breaking silence about this dangerous assumption. We've used the word "patriot" for a very long time to include both men and women. It was time to break this silence, I thought—time to use "matriot," which comes from the Latin word *mater*, to include both men and women, and to re-define what national defense might mean. So I made up the word, created the definition and the poem.

Have you ever seen or experienced something unjust? Something that has bothered you for a while, that you've not yet written about, perhaps not even spoken about? It's time to break this silence. Witness that moment that you can't forget. Write a social action poem that is burning to be written.

Charles Harper Webb

The Death of Santa Claus

He's had chest pains for weeks,
but doctors don't make house
calls to the North Pole,

he's let his Blue Cross lapse,
blood tests make him faint,
hospital gowns always flap

open, waiting rooms upset
his stomach, and it's only
indigestion anyway, he thinks,

until, feeding the reindeer,
he feels as if a monster fist
has grabbed his heart and won't

stop squeezing. He can't
breathe, and the beautiful white
world he loves goes black,

and he drops on his jelly belly
in the snow and Mrs. Claus
tears out of the toy factory

wailing, and the elves wring
their little hands, and Rudolph's
nose blinks like a sad ambulance

light, and in a tract house
in Houston, Texas, I'm eight,
telling my mom that stupid

kids at school say Santa's a big
fake, and she sits with me
on our purple-flowered couch,

and takes my hand, tears
in her throat, the terrible
news rising in her eyes.

The Author Speaks!

This poem began as a kind of cruel joke: imagining a cartoon Santa dying of a heart attack. At first, I combined medical facts with stock imagery of "Jolly Old St. Nick" at the North Pole. But, as often happens in my work, the poem turned darker as I wrote. By the time it shifts from the North Pole to Houston, it has become an elegy. I mourn the deaths of all kindly old gentlemen, and, by extension, of everyone. I mourn the loss of Santa in my life. And I mourn the loss of my own innocence, which my mother so clearly mourned.

You'll notice that I don't pretend the speaker is fictional, though, in many poems, the speaker is. Any distant memory will contain elements of fiction, simply because memory can be inaccurate. Still, as much as I can make it, I am the "me" in the poem.

Bart Edelman

Buffalo Dreams

I leave my window open
To hear the wounded buffalo
Who cannot be contained,
Forever banished by edict
From the range of the Great Plains.

The bellows arrive after midnight
When I'm settled in snuggly,
But I rise out of bed
And welcome the beast
I pray to each night.

Slowly, with cautious steps,
The huge creature appears,
Bathed in his own shadow
And the glow moonlight casts
Under a halo of stars.

In my backyard he stops
To munch the tufts of grass
And lay his burden at my feet—
The journey fraught with exhaustion,
He falls into listless sleep.

Gentle and wise is the buffalo.
Weak and wicked are the men
Foolish enough to condemn him
To wander the native land
Where America dreams no more.

The Author Speaks!

"Buffalo Dreams" is a poetic lament, of sorts. It calls into question the empty promises of the American spirit, especially as it regards the vast spaces of the metaphoric Great Plains. The poem employs the buffalo as a symbol and representation of those very promises which have become tired and listless over the past century. The narrator of the poem still retains some hope that the dream or promise of adventure and freedom is not extinct. By hearing and seeing the buffalo—even, perhaps, in the imagination—he or she somehow still "believes" in its spirit and heroic demeanor. I chose the spirit of the buffalo because of the respect and devotion Native Americans have paid to it. Not only would they follow the buffalo across the Great Plains, and elsewhere, but they also depended upon the buffalo for their basic survival, praying to its soul and utilizing every part of the animal, especially in the creature's death. Thus, the honor and spirit of the buffalo were preserved in a sacred pact that Native Americans reassured. The teaching of this poem can lead an instructor to discuss the tribulations of Native Americans, their plight, and the symbolic aspect of the buffalo and how it relates to Native Americans and all Americans (not only students) who dream of the promise of both renewal and hope.

Questions:
1. Why is the buffalo in the poem wounded?
2. What is an "edict" and why does it come "From the range of the Great Plains"?
3. Why is the narrator settled snuggly in bed?
4. Why does the narrator "welcome the beast"?
5. Why does the creature appear "Slowly, with cautious steps"?
6. What is the buffalo's burden? The narrator's?
7. What makes the buffalo "Gentle and wise"?
8. What keeps the men "Weak and wicked"?
9. Why does America dream no more?

10. Is the buffalo a symbol, and, if so, what does it represent?
11. Discuss the definition and importance of symbols, especially in poetry.

Sholeh Wolpé

My Brother at the Canadian Border

On their way to Canada in a red Mazda, my brother and his friend, PhDs and little sense, stopped at the border and the guard leaned forward, asked: *Where you boys heading?* My brother, *Welcome to Canada* poster in his eyes replied: *Mexico.* The guard blinked, stepped back then forward, said: *Sir, this is the Canadian border.* My brother turned to his friend, grabbed the map from his hands, slammed it on his shaved head. *You stupid idiot*, he yelled, *you've been holding the map upside down.*
In the interrogation room full of metal desks and chairs with wheels that squeaked and florescent light humming, bombarded with questions, and finally: *Race?*
Stymied, my brother confessed: *I really don't know, my parents never said*, and the woman behind the desk widened her blue eyes to take in my brother's olive skin, hazel eyes, the blonde fur that covered his arms and legs. Disappearing behind a plastic partition, she returned with a dusty book, thick as War and Peace, said:
This will tell us your race. Where was your father born? She asked, putting on her horn-rimmed glasses. *Persia*, he said. *Do you mean I-ran?*
I ran, you ran, we all ran, he smiled. *Where's your mother from?* Voice cold as a gun.
Russia, he replied. She put one finger on a word above a chart in the book, the other on a word at the bottom of the page, brought them together looking like a mad mathematician bent on solving the crimes of zero times zero divided by one. Her fingers stopped on a word. Declared: *You are white.*

My brother stumbled back, a hand on his chest, eyes wide, mouth in an O as in *O my God! All these years and I did not know.* Then to the room, to the woman and the guards: *I am white. I can go anywhere. Do anything. I can go to Canada and pretend it's Mexico. At last, I am white and you have no reason to keep me here.*

The Author Speaks!

This is a prose poem. A prose poem is written in the format of prose, but employs the rhythmic flow and the poetic imagery and figures used in free verse.

Is this a funny or a serious poem? What do you think of the two characters traveling to Canada? Why doesn't the immigration officer laugh at their obvious joke and wave them along?

The poet's brother's response to the question of race is that his "parents never said." Could it be that because of his "mixed race" he does not know where he belongs in a world sharply defined by racial divides? Could there be other reasons?

What do you think of the woman behind the desk who believes she can define the man's race by looking it up in a book? How does the poet portray the woman?

"My Brother at the Canadian Border" uses the comedy of the situation to make the reader comfortable before delivering a serious message. Sometimes comedy can bring down the shield put up by the reader's preconceived notions or prejudices. Once that shield is down, the reader is in a better position to receive the poem's message with a greater generosity and a more open mind.

Finally, read the poem out loud. Can you hear the internal music of the language employed? How many ways can you read this poem? Try acting out the characters.

Deena Metzger

Something in the Belly

I wanted to have a poem and I was pregnant. I was very thin. As if I'd lived on air. A poet must be able to live on air, but a mother must not attempt it. My mother wanted me to buy a set of matching pots, Wearever aluminum, like the ones she had. They were heavy and had well fitting lids so my suppers wouldn't burn. My husband wanted me to give dinner parties. John F. Kennedy was running for office.

I sensed danger. Kennedy wasn't against the Bomb or for nuclear disarmament. I joined SANE at its inception. Also Concerned Scientists. I spoke with Linus Pauling and encouraged my husband to help his partner organize Physicians for Social Responsibility.

There was a baby in my belly. I wanted to write poems. I had a crazy idea that a woman could write a real novel, the kind that shook the world. I hallucinated that a woman could be a poet, but she would have to be free. And I couldn't imagine that freedom for myself even though I could see it in Isla Negra when I followed Pablo Neruda. I could see it in the way he walked. Even if he were walking inside a dictatorship, among guns, soldiers and spies, there was nothing between him and his vision. Anything he saw, he was able to take into himself—there was no sight, no image, no vision to which he didn't feel entitled. In his heart, everything—everything—belonged to him. Pablo Neruda was—more than anything—a poet, and so he was an entitled man.

I was a woman and entitled to nothing. I had nothing except a husband, a rented house, a set of pots, living room furniture, a frenzy of obligations, credit cards, anxious relatives, too many acquaintances, a gift of future diaper service, two telephones, no time to read, a plastic wrapped cookbook of recipes gleaned from the pages of the New York Times, and a hunger, a terrible hunger for the unimaginable, unlimited freedom of being a poet, and a baby in my belly.

I would have called Pablo long distance if I had the courage, if I had the ability to speak Spanish fluently, if we had ever talked about real things. But, what would a man know about a baby in the belly? And what did it matter if there were to be one poet more or less in the world when so many in his country were dying?

I woke up one morning and thought—I can't have this child. My husband said, "You'll have to get a job after it's born so we can buy a house. You'll need an advanced degree so you can do something." I thought, I can't. I have to write a poem. My mother found a crib. Someone painted it white. A friend sent a pastel mobile with tame wood animals. I thought about blue curtains, making bedspreads and abortions.

Pablo was silent. He was walking so far away from me, I couldn't hear him. My husband objected to donating more free medical care to the Black Panthers. I tried to make *dolmades* from scratch and located grape leaves preserved in brine at the Boys' Market twenty miles away. I organized a write-in campaign against JFK and for peace. My husband thought it would be nice to have teatime with the children and romantic dinners by ourselves. The new formula bottles lined up on the sink like tiny bombs. The U.S. was pursuing overground testing; I was afraid the radiation would cross the milk barrier. I had a poem in me howling for real life but no language to write in. The fog came in thick, flapping about my feet like blankets unraveling. I became afraid to have a daughter.

I called Pablo Neruda in the middle of the night as he walked underwater by Isla Negra. He moved like a dream porpoise. He seemed pregnant with words. They came out of him in long miraculous strings. The sea creatures quivered with joy. I said, "Pablo, I want to know how to bear the child in my belly onto this bed of uranium and I want to know if a woman can be a poet." He was large as a whale.

He drank the sea and spouted it in glistening odes, black and shiny. I said, "I can't have this child," and he laughed as if he had never done anything but carry and birth children.

So I packed my little bag as if I were going to the hospital and I left a note and the Wearever pots and sterilized nipples upon the glass missiles, and took the cradle board which a Native American friend had given me for the baby and which had made my husband snort "You're not going to carry the thing on your back, are you?" I took some money, the car, some books, paper and pens, my walking shoes, an unwieldy IBM electric typewriter, my pregnant belly and a dozen cloth diapers, and I went out.

I knew how to carry a baby and how to carry a poem and would learn how to have a baby and even how to have a poem. I would have enough milk for both, and I would learn how to walk with them. But I didn't know, and didn't want to know, how to have a husband and a matched set of Wearever pots.

The Author Speaks!

This poem came from a writing assignment I gave my adult students. For ten consecutive weeks, we were to imagine that we had had a deep friendship with a writer or artist who had become important to us in our lives. We were asked to imagine how our lives would be different if we had had that friendship when were eighteen or twenty, at formative times. One could choose anyone as long as they were no longer alive.

I had always been interested in the poetry and life of Pablo Neruda. When he died several weeks after a cruel coup, *el glopé* (the blow), partially engineered by the CIA in 1973 in which General Augusto Pinochet overthrew the democratically elected government of Salvador Allende, I was heartbroken. The years that Allende had governed had resulted in the flowering of the arts, literature, and hope. People had begun to imagine freedom, and now it was gone. On September 11, 1973, artists, teachers, workers, activists were gathered in the National stadium, tortured, killed, imprisoned. Pablo Neruda, the great poet, died of heartbreak.

The assignment for this particular poem was to imagine that I had telephoned Neruda at a critical time in my life and asked for advice.

In the poem series *Walking with Neruda*, I was exploring what it means to be a poet, but especially what it means for a woman to be a poet. In the sixties and seventies, feminism called women to struggle for economic and political equality. But to gain these, women understood that they had to have respect as women, they recognized that the culture that women had created was as valuable as the dominant culture, and they had to have the ability to determine their own lives. Feminism also asserted that war was a product of patriarchy.

This poem refers to the time when John F. Kennedy was running for president and people, including women, felt similar hope to the hope experienced by people in Chile at the time of Allende. The hope was dashed, however, by Kennedy's refusal to come out for nuclear disarmament and against the use of the Atom Bomb.

The protagonist of the poem is not deciding between being a mother and being a poet. She is wondering what kind of life feeds and sustains a poet. We can imagine that she is at her wit's end when she calls the poet. He does not advise her to yield to the domestic situation. He calls her to the poet's life of freedom, commitment, and responsibility.

Lisa Russ Spaar

Hallowe'en

On the night of skulled gourds,
of small, masked demons
begging at the door,
a man cradles his eldest daughter
in the family room. She's fourteen,
she's dying because she will not eat
anymore. The doorbell keeps ringing;
his wife gives the sweets away.
He rubs the scalp
through his girl's thin hair.
She sleeps. He does not know
what to do.
When the carved pumpkin
gutters in the windowglass,
his little son races through the room,
his black suit printed with bones
that glow in the dark.
His pillowsack bulges with candy,
and he yelps with joy.
The father wishes he were young.
He's afraid of the dream
she's burning back to,
his dream of her before her birth,
so pure, so perfect,
with no body to impede her light.

The Author Speaks!

If you were to film this poem, not much would happen, at least not outwardly. It is Hallowe'en, and while trick-or-treaters ring the doorbell and his wife gives out the candy, a father "cradles," as though she were a child, his 14-year-old daughter who "will not eat any more." While he holds her in the "family room," rubbing her hair, a candle gutters in a window-reflected jack-o'-lantern, and the girl's little brother runs through the room, dressed in a skeleton costume, whooping joyfully and carrying a pillow sack full of sweets. That's it. And yet so much is happening inside the father. His daughter's anorexia is critical. It has reduced her to the catatonic sleep of an infant and has thrown his life into a crisis ("He does not know / what to do"). The girl's self-starvation is suggested in ironic, striking contrast to the "playful" images of death that characterize the holiday of Hallowe'en ("skulled gourds" and "masked demons" and the "little son . . . / his black suit printed with bones / that glow in the dark"). The poem seems to suggest that only the young, the innocent, can play at death. The father, confronted with the complexity of his daughter's illness, "wishes he were young." As she belongs less and less to her body, he recalls with irony and fear "the dream / she's burning back to, / his dream of her before her birth, / so pure, so perfect, / with no body to impede her light." The poem concludes with an expression of the manifold ways it is both difficult and joyful to live in a body. The son, daughter, mother, and father all experience this in different ways in the poem, but it is the father's anguish that is the real story of the poem and the focus of its own necessarily impeded light.

Greg Sanders

My Virtual Window

Therese told me that the one thing she'd been thinking about, regarding my small apartment, was that it was too dark, that more sunlight, a better sighting down onto the street below, would make me feel more a part of the world. You see, my little studio apartment had only one very small window. It looked north across the narrow street and it didn't bring in much light. I had a view of a vertical sliver of the city and that was about it. This was mostly due to the fact that a residential behemoth had been built in the lot across the street, and it blotted out just about everything. My apartment is on the northwest corner of the building, a red brick six-story tenement built around 1900, and if only there were a window on the west wall I'd get a lot more light. And a view. Just as Therese said, I'd feel more a part of the world.

Knowing her as well as I do, as my girlfriend, my best buddy, my confidante, I should have known that Therese would not complain about a situation without proposing a remedy. Thus, one day about three weeks ago, she texted me at work to say that tonight would be special, that she had a gift for me. As you might expect, I left at five on the dot.

When I got home, she was already there, toolkit opened, large cardboard box knocked flat, its contents spread about the floor.

"I'm glad you're here," she said. "Now I can get started."

"What is all of this?" I was delighted to see so much disarray.

But she wouldn't answer me.

"First thing is to get the steel sleeve installed," was all she said. She pulled a cordless electric drill out of her backpack with a very long 3/16" drill bit. She stepped back and squinted until she was satisfied that she'd found the appropriate spot on the wall. "Here," she said, with a bit of triumph, pressing her pinky against said spot. Revving the drill to its max RPM, she drove the bit through the plaster, through the lathing, into a couple of layers of bricks (the bit smoking and squealing now), then she pulled it out, poured some water on it, and set it back in. She pressed the trigger and leaned on the drill until the bit pushed through to the outside world.

I should say that I love watching my girl handling tools. It's a funny thing to say, true, but you'd say the same thing if you saw Therese with that electric drill in her hand. She's got long, elegant fingers, and the tendons that make them work run up her forearms like piano wires. When she moves her fingers, they move too. To my eyes, it's like a fine sonata. She simply has this innate confidence when it comes to handling things in the physical world. Once, when we'd just started dating, we volunteered to help my grandparents rebuild a part of their deck. They've got this old country place in the boondocks and are dead broke. Well that weekend was when my heart began to ache for Therese, when I saw how she handled a hammer, the way she put the nails between her teeth, three or four at a time, getting them queued up to go into her left hand, and then with her right she'd strike that nail perfect the very first time. Bang, bang, bang, and it was seated in the pressure-treated one-by-four and soon my grandparents' deck was nicely patched and my girl, the future love of my life, had a little sweat stain going down her back.

Now, back to the installation of my gift. As noted, she'd punched through the entire wall, not the kind of thing my landlord would be thrilled about.

"You are out of your mind," I said, and I still believe that it's half true.

She held before my eyes a little metal tube—this was the sleeve—and forced it, twisting it all the while, through the long narrow hole to the outside world. She stopped before the tube vanished entirely, leaving maybe two inches sticking out of the wall. Holding it in place, she used the heel of the electric drill to tap a flange into it. Into the flanged tube she threaded the fiber optic cable with the tiny lens on the end. Now a tail of fiber optic cable hung from the wall, looking like a rodent's tail. She used some lead mollies and bolts to mount two brackets on the wall.

I should mention that I did offer to help, but she just wiped her dark hair away from her eyes and told me to stay put, that this was a present and I must not interfere. Then came the virtual window itself. She attached the tail of fiber optic cable to a node on its back, hung it on the brackets, unraveled its electric cable, and plugged it into the wall outlet above the baseboard.

"Do the honors?" she said, and I pressed the button on the front of the window.

And by god, like a miniature miracle, there on my wall hung a clear view of the outside world. She flipped through the instruction manual and adjusted some settings displayed on the screen. The last thing she did was snap faux muntins into place over the window so that now it really looked like a window.

She sat on the bed next to me, her body warm, her fingers covered in brick dust and, like a pair of ironic hipsters, we immersed ourselves in the image of the moment instead of the moment itself. We skated along the surface of the emotions instead of immersing ourselves in them. For close to five minutes we remained cowering in a vacuum of silence, until I thanked her, and told her I loved her.

Last week I noticed a peculiarity about my virtual window. Things always seemed brighter, somehow hopeful compared with the way they appeared when I looked outside of the small, pathetic (yet very real) window. Through the real window I'd see roiling clouds, and haze would be obscuring the horizon. I'd see the incinerator flu of a far off building spewing black smoke into the air. Then, looking outside via the virtual window, the sky would be a bit less cloudy, the air clear, and I swear even the people walking down on the street seemed to be happier, lighter on their feet than I'd ever seen in reality. I asked my girl exactly what kind of a window she'd installed. "Oh, that. Well it's the Optimist's tint. I turned it on because you seemed a bit depressed, and I thought it'd be nice to cheer you up a bit." I found out how to navigate to the tint settings and turned off the Optimist's setting so now, at last, I can look at my wall, at the once blank facade that would do nothing but stare back at me, and I can see the world below nearly as it is, and I am beginning to think I am dating a genius.

The Author Speaks!

With "My Virtual Window" I wanted to experiment with creating a story out of what is essentially an installation guide for a fictitious (but perhaps not unreasonable) piece of hardware. I wanted to have some fun with the romantic relationship between the narrator and his girlfriend, as well, and to counter some clichés vis-à-vis a woman "doing a man's work." The pleasure of writing this story had to do with imagining the mechanical details of installing this device (don't try this at home!) and how it might affect the relationship between the narrator and his girlfriend.

Erinn Batykefer

Allegheny Love Letter

As the knife is made to cut, I can be nothing
less than I am, and so I will be honest:
I have no memory, and I am always running

away. Even after rain, when my skin is glass
and I reflect back everything you say, already
a dam is opening upstream to wash you away.

You know this, as you must know that in me,
eyeless, limivorous fishes dig food from the muck
among rotting suicides, that every flood

has me spilling sewage and gore over my banks.
And still, there you are among sycamores or waving
from bridges. Like a fool you carry me with you

in the volume of your skin like a photo;
green veins tattoo a map of me over your wrists.
You must know that if I love you back

it will be at sixty-thousand cubic feet per second.
This is not meander, not the slow lave of an oxbow.
This is ark and animals scrambling

for high ground, eyes rolling. Below the surface,
my current gathers itself into what I really am:
amnesiac, unmerciful. I will sweep you away,

and when you are gone, in relentless grief
I will flood my banks to touch the earth where you stood,
and wash them down to bedrock.

The Author Speaks!

When I started writing an early draft of this poem, I was trying to express an intense but destructive kind of love by likening the intensity of such an emotion to a powerful natural phenomenon: a river flooded with spring rain. The river I chose is a river I learned to row on when I was in high school, the Allegheny, which runs through Pittsburgh, Pennsylvania, and so the landscape of the poem is a Pittsburgh/Western PA landscape. Through progressive drafts, I found that the speaker of the poem wasn't just describing his or her feelings through the metaphor of a flooded river, but was speaking as the river itself. And so, this final draft is written in the voice of the Allegheny River.

Cecile Rossant

Real Estate

Lily wants to build a house on P.'s estate.

P. has already built three beautiful houses on his large property. Two of these are relatively small structures, while the third is middling to large.

Lily lives on a property that is part of a new estate. Its group of four houses is well planned and effectively coordinated.

Real estate is not all that attractive to Lily or P. but neither he nor she has avoided the business altogether.

In fact, if they travel together, they stay at hotels and tend not to concern themselves with the details of managing their respective estates.

P. needs to build a small shed to house his many tools. Because Lily is familiar with P.'s property, P. finds it useful to discuss his plans with her. As it is being built, the shed appears house-like. This continues to be the case even after all of P.'s tools are in place.

Lily wants to put up a tent on P.'s property. P. puts up no protest, but Lily doesn't follow through with her plans. "In my tent," she says, "I would always be anticipating impressions; I'd imagine a threat where there would actually be none—"

No one would understand her living in a tent and sleeping in a house.

Lily can always visit P.'s estate by bringing herself over in broad daylight. P.'s property is only deceptively large and uncultivated.

One fateful morning, Lily leaves all the windows of her house open. Wind blows through, gnawing at the walls. Various pieces break away and are blown to different positions in the house.

Lily leaves all the water faucets running. Her basins overflow. The floorboards at first blackened and wet through are soon looking up through a layer of water.

Water stains creep up the papered walls.

She enters the kitchen. Much debris has landed on the stovetop. The flame from one of four burners is enough to play havoc.

Lily is already running to P.'s estate as the three other houses burst into flames.

She enters one of his houses, opens all the windows, the faucets, and her flame-throwing mouth.

The fire burns—Lily wakes up under the open sky inhaling the acrid smell of wet ashes deeply into her nose. Upon standing, she notices a stream crossing the property that she had overlooked before.

Lily walks along its edge. The walking brings her back to her property—she turns around and walks back to his. She continues walking back and forth, property to property, until she must finally sit down from exhaustion.

Her eyes relax on the water. She lets a hand dangle and cause a braid of ripples.

She feels for the slippery mud beneath the mat of leaves.

The Author Speaks!

There are some things we cannot talk about directly, so we use a kind of code. We encrypt our story in a metaphor that has meaning and a direct reference for us, but perhaps others will only sense the emotion in our story or its pattern, plot, and development without knowing the actual context—what it means to us. The reader might guess at a reference for the metaphor and hopefully find one in his or her own life. In this way we can resolve a dilemma or problem we might have by "getting to the end of the story" or simply telling the story without endangering ourselves by relating it with proper names, facts, and details. "Real Estate" uses this means of encryption.

Ron Koertge

Cinderella's Diary

I miss my stepmother. What a thing to say
but it's true. The prince is so boring: four
hours to dress and then the cheering throngs.
Again. The page who holds the door is cute
enough to eat. Where is he once Mr. Charming
kisses my forehead goodnight?

Every morning I gaze out a casement window
at the hunters, dark men with blood on their
boots who joke and mount, their black trousers
straining, rough beards, callused hands, selfish,
abrupt...

Oh, dear diary—I am lost in ever after:
those insufferable birds, someone in every
room with a lute, the queen calling me to look
at another painting of her son, this time
holding the transparent slipper I wish
I'd never seen.

The Author Speaks!

I seem to be fatally attracted to heroes and heroines in fairy tales and comic books and movies. Over the years I've written about Superman and Dracula and King Kong and dozens of others. Students sometimes think that poets have mostly lofty thoughts. Not me. And if I have a lofty thought I try to get rid of it fast so something more interesting can get in.

    I love the "What If?" principle in writing and use it all the time. What if Cinderella wasn't happy in Ever After? What if King Kong escaped with the blonde? What if Hester in *The Scarlet Letter* was proud of her A? What if the Seven Dwarfs got tired of having Snow White around? Write your own "What If?" poem.

DeWitt Henry

Odd

The oddest adult in my suburban Philadelphia childhood was a retired prizefighter, a man blinded in the ring, but someone who had had a serious career and earned a fortune, so that he lived with his sister and his German wolfhounds in a forty or fifty-room mansion that we, my friends and I and other schoolchildren, passed each day walking to and from school.

For me, the walk home each afternoon was one mile, the length of Midland Avenue from Louella, past the single-floor "modern" house with picture windows on the right, past the Catholic school where tough kids hung out, past Bob Teal's house on the left (his father, Mr. Teal, was the high school music teacher and band leader, and Bob's two older sisters were cheerleaders), then the long uphill block to St. David's Avenue. Mostly I walked with Dale Wilson, who lived in the new apartments on the corner of St. David's Avenue and Lancaster Pike; we walked, careful not to step on sidewalk cracks, and talked about how babies arrived. Dale had the idea that it had something to do with sex, but I disagreed, horrified at the idea, and said what my mother had said, which was that when a man and woman loved each other and were together for a while, then a baby happened. We were ten. 1952. TV was still a luxury. At school we practiced air raid drills in basement hallways lined with civil defense boxes and canisters. At home, one of my favorite toys was a model of a B-52 bomber that released an atomic bomb when I pushed a button on top.

There were kids, other ages, who walked the same street, and the legend had spread that halfway up the long uphill block was the house where this retired fighter lived, who loved kids. That any afternoon if you braved the white gate between the solid bank of hedges and pine trees that sheltered the view of his home from the street; if you ventured up his strange front walk to the wooden porch; if you braved the first floor windows flanking the front door; if you rang the button bell and had the nerve to wait, as if for trick or treat—first, there would be the dogs barking, throaty woofs muffled by the house, then, perhaps, a woman's voice:

"Quiet! Quiet! Just a minute, I'm coming."

And the sounds of her presence, a blurred face peering, the unlocking and opening of the oak front door into a paneled vestibule.

Dale had done it twice before he told me. Other kids had taken him. As we came up the hill, he urged me to try; did I want a candy bar or not? For that was the prize.

The lady who answered would be gray-haired, tall, formally dressed. She would materialize before you, questioning, as if she had no idea: "Yes?"

And you would say that you had heard that the man here liked to meet children.

And she would answer: "Yes, yes, just a minute."

Perhaps from the strange depths of the inner hall and the house's reaches and darkness, a deeper, gravelly man's voice would be calling: "Sonja. Sonja? Who is it? Who's there?"

"It's some children!" she would call. And then to you: "Just a minute. He'll want to meet you."

There would be a shuffling behind her and this man, casually dressed, a handsome man larger than any father, broad shouldered, broad faced, wearing slacks and an ascot and with neatly combed white hair, would emerge, and she would make way. You would be scared but at the same time fascinated to look: the face, the eyes, the blank, cloudy, unseeing eyes. The face handsome otherwise, like Wallace Beery's, the actor's, or like Ralph Bellamy's; an educated and distinguished face. And he would be tapping with his cane and groping forward.

"Hello," he'd say. "Are these the children?" And then to you, "Hello," he'd say to space, the space where you, the unknown, waited. "What's your name? How many, two? What are your names?"

And you might find the nerve to answer, or your friend might; for no kid would ever try this alone, except for maybe Shaner, the older kid who had first brought Dale here, and from whom, perhaps, the man's rumored history had begun. Whatever first had led Shaner here, a meeting on the street, some door-to-door solicitation, Shaner had had the nerve to ask: How did you get blinded? In the ring, the man answered. Perhaps Shaner had been inside. Were there trophies inside? Pictures on the walls? Clippings in a scrapbook? How did we know the lady to be the man's sister?

"Have you been here before?" the man would ask.

"No, never. Just some kids told us we should stop and ring the bell."

"That's right," the man says. And then: "And you? What's your name?"

"Dee," I say uncertainly, for I *am* there; but at the same time I relax, because so far this all seems rehearsed, a customary thing, and going just the way Dale has said.

"Tell me some things you like to do," the man says. "Do you like sports?"

"Football."

"Hmmm," he says. "You an Eagles fan?"

"Sure am," I lie.

"What are your favorite subjects in school?"

I say art. Dale says math.

"Hmmm. Here's a riddle for you. Let's see: What goes up the chimney down, but can't go down the chimney up?" He turns his face expectantly from one of us to the other.

I have heard the riddle before, but never really understood the answer.

"C'mon, guess. You've heard this one."

"Santa? I don't know."

He chuckled. "An umbrella."

Dale and I look at each other.

He smiles broadly. "You're good children. I can tell," he congratulates us. "Can I feel your faces?"

I stand confused, for Dale has never mentioned this, but I can't refuse, or probably the man won't give us the candy. So I let him touch, his coarse fighter's fingers drifting delicately over my features.

~

A lifetime later, that blind man's gentle, rapid touch, searching my features, haunts my imagination. Dismissing any suggestion of perversion (as our parents must have dismissed it then), I have come to think that for him the touch was redemptive.

Perhaps sixty at the time, he must have fought as a young man some thirty years before, in the era if not that of Gentleman Jim Corbett, then that of Jack Dempsey, Gene Tunney, and the Frenchman Georges Carpentier, and those very hands, as fists, had beaten men senseless, scores of men, men who had been intent, too, on battering him unconscious, all for the diversion of thousands of fans in echoing, smoky arenas, on from the 1920s into the Depression years.

I try to imagine such a man's life. Whether his wealth was partly inherited and he had come from a privileged background (and if so, what had driven him to fight, what buried rage, or what further need to prove his superiority against those who challenged it in physical, rather than in social terms). Whether he had gone to a private men's academy, like my older brothers, and started boxing in school; then had gone on to college at some place like Yale, Cornell, or Princeton, and boxed there. Had moved from school to amateur bouts, had turned professional and worked his way through ranks of street pugs and men from backgrounds that offered no means for livelihood or gain but this, men fighting for survival and advancement.

Or whether he himself had been poor. Had never been to college. Had labored and battled and suffered like the prizefighters in Hollywood films. Had from teens through his twenties battled not only opponents' fists, but also the greed of gamblers, molls, and promoters. Had had the sense to save and invest his winnings. And then what fight had ended his career? Perhaps he hadn't been blinded in the ring at all. Perhaps some gangsters had blinded him.

Somehow, I imagine, his money had cost not only his eyes but also his dignity; that he had felt some shame for his past. Perhaps in years of bitterness he had come to reflect on the squalor of violence. On the savageness of man.

He was a man without a wife and children. The house and grounds, in our town, must have been worth sixty or seventy thousand dollars at the time—hardly an estate, but evidence of respectable fortune. He and his sister lived reclusively so far as we could tell. Why had they moved here, and when? Where was romance in his life? Had he lost a woman? What was his sister's story?

Perhaps they traveled regularly to Europe. He must have books in Braille, but otherwise little business in his day, little to amuse him. There he sits, listening to the radio, or to the phonograph. Perhaps he listens to recorded plays. Perhaps his sister reads to him.

For myself, I am troubled by the ugliness. Not the ugliness of his sightless gaze or searching touch; not the violence he had caused and suffered; not his adult pathos and mystery, all of which he exposed to us in his need. But by my own ugliness of submitting there to the oddness so that I could get my candy bar and escape.

～

"You are good children," he repeats. "Here is a candy bar for each of you." He gropes back into the hall. The sister has vanished. There is some sort of basket, and he offers me my choice. A Hershey's? Or a Clark Bar? Or a Mounds? I ask for the Clark. Dale takes a Hershey's. "Wait," he says, "you're such good kids. I can tell. Let me give you each two."

He does, both Hershey's this time.

"Now you come again. Come back again!" he says, shaking our hands. Patting our shoulders. Then releasing us with a wave and smile into nothingness.

"Come again."

We never do, or at least I don't, though I do tell some other kids. And later, other times, when my mother drives me on this street from school, or on our way to or from errands and shopping, I would see him sometimes from the car. He'd be out walking, with his cane, and wearing his dark glasses, his arm in his sister's, and the two wolfhounds straining on leashes. He would be dressed dapperly, scarf, cap, overcoat.

The Author Speaks!

Questions:
1. What do you consider normal and abnormal?
2. How do you come to understand a seemingly abnormal figure?

Douglas Kearney

The Orange Alert

Picture the upturned millipede, dead,
        and see the streets of Altadena:
palm tree rows against the concrete, stiff
        to the horizon.
There have been no birds big enough,
        we are comforted, to pluck
the chitins from before our yards
        and vanish
into the sun like dog-fighting MIGs.
        War bears litters of similes.

Altadena, smog hugs the foothills like mustard gas
        where our rich peer through their blinds
into ravines, Santa Anas sway the mustard plants, yuccas
        bob, some man—his cigarette,
a full gas-can, an itch. We've known
        the orange alert, fires reaching for helicopters
like cartoon cats clawing at panicked birds.

Yesterday, fire engines and HAZMAT trucks
        jostled at Alameda and El Molino
like beetles eating a four-legged spider.
        That morning, radios warned of orange.
Neighborhood kids watched officers climb in
        and out an open manhole,

consulting the entrails of the great dead millipede.
        We watched the ground;
the sun hotter than all year.
        The mountains hid Santa Anas,
the smog went orange with dusk, the growing shadows
        of lingering birds.

The Author Speaks!

Poetic license is a funny thing. It basically means that, when writing a poem, a poet can change what actually happened in order to make a poem better. It separates poetry from journalism, in which people expect to read the details of what actually happened. This poem's details are, however, true (the millipede stuff, OK, not so much).

"The Orange Alert" as a title is based on the Homeland Security Advisory System's color-coded ratings (and means high risk of terrorist attack). The poem takes place on what was, at that point, the hottest day of the year in Los Angeles County. I thought about how heat tends to magnify anxiety and tempers and how that would impact fears born of human-made and/or natural disasters.

Julie Shigekuni

The Problem with Eating Japanese

A minor fender bender on the Hollywood Freeway had slowed miles of traffic to a crawl, ensuring that Melissa would arrive late for dinner with Mark. Knowing he always got to places ahead of time for the simple reason that he hated to be kept waiting, her heart rate quickened with each passing minute. But the tardiness was not her fault, and at least Mark had his books. Lately he'd been so busy cramming for the California Bar, there was a chance he wouldn't even notice the passing time. Rushing in to the restaurant, she could see that she'd been both right and wrong. Mark was seated at the booth under the neon green *Kirin* sign that they picked whenever it was available, his head bowed over a foot high stack of papers while he slurped *gyoza* and rice from a *chawan* held under his chin.

"I don't suppose you want to share any of that," she teased, scooting onto the wooden bench across from him.

"I waited twenty minutes, then I ordered." Mark put down his *chawan* and wiped his mouth without looking up. He obviously wasn't in good humor.

He had a thing about lateness; she knew that. But she felt the same way about manners. Like not starting to eat until everyone had been served, and so she wasn't about to apologize. "I'm not that late," she reminded him, "considering traffic on the 101. I had to drive in from downtown. Remember?"

She accepted his offer of the remaining *gyoza*, but begrudgingly, her preoccupation having turned to anger. He should have waited for her, the way her stepfather always waited for her mother to sit down before starting to eat. "*Itadakimasu*," he'd say, clasping his hands.

Her mother would pull her chair under her so that she perched on the edge, a bird ready to sing. "*Doozo*," she'd say.

Melissa felt fairly confident that her mother liked Mark and knew, too, that she was right to be hesitant about him. It had taken tremendous effort on her part to ensure Asako's approval. Coaching him on manners, trying gently to inform him of her mother's way of doing things without offending him—without offending either of them. If she tended to judge him through her mother's eyes, it was out of respect for their shared values. Things like manners were important to her. If he were Japanese, it might not have mattered so much, but then, if he were Japanese, she figured he'd have good manners. Melissa understood what her mother meant when she said that people were judged by their manners. Manners made a difference. That and the fact that he'd attended their church for so many years. Melissa still remembered how Mark showed up for service with his family dressed in a suit and tie one Sunday when they were both thirteen. How miserably he stuck out. But then it turned out that his Aunt Edith, the wife of his father's brother, was Japanese.

"If we were having dinner at my mom's house you wouldn't start eating until everyone was served, would you?"

Understanding that he was being provoked, Mark finally looked up. "What? Am I on trial here?"

"No, just answer the question."

"What question, Mel? What are you talking about?"

"Just what I said. You're not going to be one of those slouches who forgets his manners once he's married, are you?"

"So you've decided to marry me?"

"Did I say that?" She had to smile because lately every conversation they had turned into a debate about marriage. Just maybe, she didn't want to get married. But the question for her wasn't really *whether* to get married, it was *when*.

"As far as I can tell, I've got the best manners in the room," Mark quipped, and Melissa tried to see the restaurant as he saw it, the black-haired men at the next table talking boisterously and loud, their fashion-conscious wives silently nodding.

"Those couples are from Japan," she whispered. "I'm not talking about the foreigners."

Mark shrugged. "I'll try to live up to your expectations of how a good *American* man should behave at the dinner table. I just never realized manners were that important to you."

She could get angry all over again that Mark had failed to recognize something so fundamentally important to her, but what would be the point? "Just promise you won't embarrass me in front of my mother."

"What?" he said, taking a moment to think. "Your mother has said I have impeccable manners."

"Okay," she sighed, forcing herself not to respond with bitterness to his self-congratulatory tone. "I'm sorry."

Mark rolled his eyes. "Maybe we shouldn't talk again until I finish reading this."

"Okay." She stared down at the tabletop, unwilling to meet Mark's eye. The fact was that she loved him, and didn't know where her dark moods came from, or why they seemed to strike out of nowhere, the way the night happens when you walk out of an afternoon matinee only to find the sun gone and you can't even remember where you parked your car. No big deal, except that for a minute you feel completely lost.

Melissa feared unhappiness and the potential for unhappiness, which was connected in her mind to Mark. She wanted to think it was because he wasn't Japanese, but she knew that was only part of it. Looking up, she followed the hum over the tabletop to the neon sign overhead responsible for casting Mark in a sickly shade of green. They would have to find a new table. The salty smell of *shoyu* and vinegar drifted in from beyond the parted *arami* curtains, and just as she was about to complain that the service was unusually slow, the same smiling waitress they always had came by for her order. Then the door chimes tinkled to announce the Kumagais from church.

"Hey!" Mark waved his arms in their direction. "Should I ask them to join us?"

"No."

But the Kumagais were already on their way over, and behind them another church couple.

"Why does this always happen when you eat Japanese?" she whispered when they were alone again. "You can't even start dinner without someone dropping by."

"No kidding, if we were going to have a fight we should have had Italian or something."

"Maybe tomorrow night." She sneered, but conceded to herself that Mark's observation had been right.

"What's wrong with you, anyway?"

Not until she'd finished her noodles and Mark had stopped leafing through his papers did she even know where to begin.

The Author Speaks!

I chose this piece because it reminded me of struggles I had when I was much younger—dating and trying to decide what was important to me in a potential partner. I don't know that I was much like Melissa, this female character, but I grew up in a traditional Japanese household, and sometimes I felt elevated because of that fact, and sometimes being Japanese was a chip on my shoulder.

This story is the beginning of a longer scene, which takes place midway into my novel, *Unending Nora*. The novel is about the disappearance of Nora Yano, and the conversation you read eventually wends its way to questions Melissa has about Nora.

Questions:
1. In what ways is racism guiding the exchange between Melissa and Mark?
2. How can you relate to Melissa when she brings up the subject of manners? What do you think she's really talking about?
3. What issues of gender are raised? How are they typical? How are they specific to the characters?
4. How important is it to this story that Melissa has been raised in a "traditional Japanese" household? What differences would it make if she were Mexican? African American? Native American? White?
5. Why do you think the author chose to use Japanese words in the conversation held between Melissa's mother and stepfather?

Lisa C. Krueger

Ballet Ghost

once she painted her dance
from memory of the studio mirror,

its silver screen a movie for one.
wielded oils in dense delicious smudges—

thumb and brush-frosted thighs
like cakes of rich peach-meat.

unabashed flesh in childhood acrylic
faded, flaked.

she no longer dances
or paints

avoids reflections
of the bone feast

skin stretched taught
against its frame,

canvas without creator,
dancer without dance.

The Author Speaks!

This poem illustrates how one girl has changed in terms of how she sees herself—from being a dancer with legs "like rich peach-meat" to a girl-ghost who looks like a "bone feast."

This poem brings up issues about growing up—how our self-perceptions can change, how we may diminish parts of ourselves to cope with the adult world we are facing.

There are many opportunities in this poem to stretch one's imagination: to envision how this girl sees herself, and then to look in our own "silver screen" to consider how each of us might have changed over time. Do you like what you see?

Shelley Savren

Yom Kippur

I

The Day of Atonement meant no food,
no water, no talking, either. Always
the hottest day in our Conservative synagogue
where Cantor Goodfriend chanted Hebrew prayers.
My sister and I played silent finger games
between all the standing and bowing. I was afraid
to go to the bathroom and miss the moment
God was forgiving me for all my bad words,
fights on the playground,
squinting my eyes in anger at Mom.

Mid afternoon, we drove to the Orthodox *shul*,
where my grandma stood behind
a curtain with Mrs. Gross and *Tanta* Lena,
the two Rose Friedmans, all of them
pounding their chests in prayer. Old women
with accents and cracked voices *davening*
in that suffocating room, casting their sins away.
I tried to go with my brother to the other side
where men could pray without the distraction
of women's shapes, where I could watch
the *Torah* come out of the ark and down the aisle,
but my grandma tucked me behind her skirt
and continued to *shuckle* and chant.

Seven *yahrzeit* candles lit her home
for two husbands dead by heart attack and stroke,
her father killed in Romania,
mother and sister at Auschwitz,
a friend with no family and one for all
the holocaust victims. *Zachar*, to remember.
Kosher wine and honey cake awaited
her long walk home in shoes that hurt her feet.
She dared not ride on *Yom Kippur* or turn
on lights, lift the phone. From sunset to sunset
nothing was permitted but prayer.

II

Yom Kippur became a ritual fast,
a day of reflection, a time to set goals.
I wanted no part in temple.
Temple was for the obedient daughter.
God would have to find me on the street.

But today I come to synagogue so my daughter
and converted husband will understand
what it means to be a Jew.
I open my prayer book, chant in unison
the litany of sins we all commit,
asking for an empty slate.
The hardest one to forgive is myself.
I have my beating stick and my wicked tongue.

Tomorrow no one in this room will be hungry.
But today I will forgive and be forgiven
because I am a Jew,
and when the *shofar* blows,
I will break my fast with cake and wine
and dip apples into honey for a sweet New Year.

The Author Speaks!

Think of a holiday celebration or a traditional family event and how it has changed for you over the years. Using your five senses and detailed imagery, tell some of that story—either focusing on yourself and how you changed over the years or on some family member who has always been there. Use lots of detailed descriptions and create pictures of scenes with your words so readers can feel like they are right there with you. Also make it sensual. In other words, use your five senses to make the scene and the people in it come alive. Let your poem recreate an experience in poetry form.

Kate Gale

Jazz is Not Enough

In a life, undoubtedly, jazz is not enough,
not enough for burnt leftover coffee grounds
not enough to keep the woman upstairs,
the woman who lived right over us,
that close. And left her man
last week, that scream still hangs in the air
and took some of his clothing
he says and a lock of his hair
though why she'd want that I don't know.
and jazz is not enough
to keep the waiters happy.
jazz does nothing for greens and rice.
does nothing.
what I've got is I'm on the outside
where I've always been,
and you're playing me music, man,
and it's not enough.
you set it up in the tv room,
and I had to laugh at that
but it wasn't happiness you understand,
and you started playing the blues
and then Bessie,
and you kept playing.
it's not enough, but sometimes
while that music is wailing,
I'll lie down and you'll hook your legs

around my legs and then it's enough.
it's all right, I tell you.
your pants over the chair
cream colored and sassy,
and me all river swim clean,
and our legs webbed together
our feet laying together like swim fins
and I'll remember the black tunnel we came through
and how when we came up for air
there was a huge rush of sunlight
and how you smiled
and then the music
and then it's enough
with your legs and my legs
mixed up and the quilt
with pieces from so many places
I can't remember.

The Author Speaks!

Write about a type of music you love to listen to when you are trying to relax and get away from your problems. What does it make you think about? Why do you feel comfortable with it? Sometimes you want someone to love your music, too, because then you feel you know them better. That's part of what we do when we fall in love.

Gaylord Brewer

The Bath

My favorite scene in any Western
is when the trail-boss or prospector
arrives grizzled and stinking
after a long tango with wilderness.
He sees his horse watered, fed, brushed,
then makes a dusty entrance
at the hotel-*cum*-saloon. Next shot,
a middle-aged firecracker in a bustier,

Big Red or Miss Betty and still
more than *you* can handle, believe it,
is reading the fellow hell
as she twists off each cracked boot
and peels away the soiled layers
no lady should have to see.
Then cut to the guy's bony shoulders
above an iron tub and the next bucket

of boiling water, *whoo-ee*,
right over his mangy head.
What's a man to do except bellow
like the devil and secretly love it?
When we meet again, he is grotesquely
transformed: beard clipped,
wet hair combed back to a duck's tail,
stiff and scratchy in clean duds.

There's gold in his vest
for the whole bottle, and this town's
a raucous nest of possibilities—
some crooked cards, a sweet missy
to snuggle, a soft and civilized bed.
Sadly, that's when the doors fly off
and some goon's young brother,
finger twitching, sidles on in.

The Author Speaks!

We're movie people. Most of us have grown up watching films and loving them. In "The Bath," I pick a silly scene that I feel like I've seen a million times, played by Robert Mitchum or Jack Elam or Ernest Borgnine or lots of other old actors you probably haven't heard of. It's a small moment but, I think, an important one about coming in from the remote frontier, rejoining society, and having mixed feelings over the compromise. What other scenes in movies do we tell to ourselves over and over as a culture? Write a poem beginning with the line, "My favorite scene in any ____" and fill in the blank on the movie genre. Science fiction? Fantasy? Horror? Spy? Boy Meets Girl? (You might try casting an actor or actress against type—Hugh Grant as a slasher!?—and having fun with what you discover from the clash.) Flesh out the narrative scene, employing/enjoying the stereotypes and exploring whatever message or warning the story might symbolize.

Sholeh Wolpé

The Deep Dive

Stevie's raisin-colored braids,
 a shade lighter than his skin,
bob up–down as the waves punch the boat.

He signals *Go down*.
I don't.

I stay close to the boat,
hold tight the taut rope.
                        Can't breathe.
Not the air in the tank.
Not the air in the air.
My lungs inflate, deflate,
but that's beside the point.
                        I can't freakin' breathe,
and I yell this to the waves,
to the boat,
to Stevie
who magically surfaces beside me,
an aurous brown god in goggles,
regulator hose dangling by his mouth.
He holds my head between his palms, says,
                      "But you ARE breathing. You ARE."

I look at him and even in this panic, this feeling
of imminent death, I note how beautiful he is,
how I could perhaps outlive this storm

in this man's brawny arms, let myself go
and the heck with the world,
with who I am, or am supposed to be,
with my anxious lover waiting at the shore.

"Relax, baby," says Stevie, "I'll stay with you."
He pulls me into his arms and I breathe deep
from the tank strapped to my back. Stealthily
he releases air from my jacket, adds
a cube of weight to my belt ,
and down we go, down
into the broth of another world.

The sea bottom is a sandy desert flush against massive rocks,
and there are cacti, tiny Joshua trees, and brown grass dancing
to the water current's silent tango . . .
Time means nothing here.
Palestine, Israel, and Tehran mean nothing here,
my daughter contemplating suicide at twelve means nothing here,
sons in military fatigue breathing Iraqi air means nothing here,
even women giving life and grenades taking them away,
mean nothing here.

Here, the fish are birds,
electric blue fins, wings,
and beneath this airless sky, Stevie and I.

The Author Speaks!

A poem can begin one place and take you someplace else . . . somewhere totally unexpected. "The Deep Dive" begins with the poet in choppy waters. She is obviously not a very experienced diver, yet is experienced enough to have thought she could handle the rough weather.

Soon you are allowed to enter deeper into her mind—see the way she sees the dive master, feel her sudden new (though imaginary) relationship with him. From the way she is devising a fantasy escape from her own life into a safe world with the handsome dive master, you can begin to surmise the world she may be coming from. A world that is perhaps not very safe and happy. Stevie offers her air and comfort. Does he represent anything or anyone for the poet?

Two-thirds into the poem, she and Stevie sink into "the broth of another world." What does that mean? Is this just a physical shift, or is it a psychological one as well? How does that afford her a new perspective on her own life and of the world she lives in. Have you ever experienced such a shift in perspective when flying in an airplane?

Does the poet finally find the escape she desperately needs through a shift in perspective?

Elizabeth Bradfield

Pilgrimage Midsummer

Beautiful, in fog, to find and lose
the trail, the view, blueberries
low against rock. Road sound
for a while out of mind. We'd driven

hours to get here, pitched our tent
alongside others come for reasons
that couldn't be too different. But
we thought we'd lost them all,

congratulated ourselves for rising
early, choosing a trail marked *difficult*
and then going by topo-map
and gut alone. So it's no surprise

that when we scrambled up the back slope
of the park's highest peak and met
the rest of America, who'd driven up
a road we didn't know was there, hate

made us hungry. We slouched
through the parking lot to the snack bar,
tore open a bag of salt and vinegar chips,
chewed and glowered. What made us think

this view, this day was somehow stolen from us?
Kids were jumping rock-to-rock, popsicles
sticky down their wrists, laughing. We took a picture
leaving all that out. We walked back down.

The Author Speaks!

Have you ever planned a day and found yourself disappointed when it didn't turn out as you expected? It could be me, but this, to my mind, is a common occurrence. As a naturalist, I spend a lot of time on trails and in the woods. I lead people on hikes and kayaking trips and I am there to teach them about the plants and animals, to be an expert. Often, I find that at the beginning of a walk or a trip, there is a restlessness, a nervousness that nothing "amazing" will happen. In this poem, I wanted to explore that frustration of expectation at my own expense.

This poem is deliberately in conversation with other poems that chronicle walks in the woods where the speaker has some moment of communion with a coyote, bear, bird, or plant. Obviously, there's no rapture here, though. Instead of a bear, the hikers got a parking lot of RVs. Instead of birdcalls, they got kids playing. I think this is a fairly typical experience, but one that isn't often seen in poetry. It's a poem that pokes fun at the smug nature-lover who can gush over a flower but will turn surly upon seeing other people. Why do we have such strange divisions between the natural world and the social world?

Ed Falco

Faith

In the dark in the no-light at the field's center. Cows. Two cows. This is about what I believe. There are two cows in the center of a field that I can not see. Two cows in the dark. I attribute my belief to a small part of the soul where knowledge resides and informs faith. That in the field there are two cows I can not see. Not-cows which I can not see. I know the cows are there because I know the owner of the field. He lives in town. He sold off the herd he said except two cows. These two cows. I know the cows are here because I can hear them. I hear them here making cow sounds which are mostly munching and chomping sounds. *Moo. Moo.* That's me. I say *Moo, Moo.* I don't know why. Sometimes I talk to myself. I tell myself to have faith. Here in the center of this dark field where I can't see a blessed thing, this seems like a good time. How did I get here? I don't know. I don't have the faintest idea. I wouldn't even swear that I'm here, it's so dark, except I hear the cows munching and I started out to cross the field. I was bored. That was before I got scared. Now I'm not bored. I'm scared because I can't see. I'm completely in the dark. It's exciting. I'm lost. Here I go. I'm walking toward what I'm sure are two cows. *Moo*, I say. So they know I'm coming.

The Author Speaks!

"Faith" is a seriously comic story about someone in a cow pasture on a pitch black night. The speaker can't see a thing, and, for reasons he himself (or she herself) seems not to know, he's (or she's) walking through darkness toward two cows. Most of this short fiction consists of speculation about what the speaker is doing and why. Readers will see quickly, however, that the situation is a comic metaphor for the role faith plays in life. The big cosmic, theological questions—Where did we come from? Where are we going? How do we know anything?—are replayed comically in this little story of someone in a cow pasture on a dark night.

The speaker in "Faith" finds herself (or himself) in the center of a field on a pitch dark night, one of those nights that happen out in the country, where you can't see your own hand in front of your face. What does that have to do with questions of faith?

Eva Saulitis

Wondering Where the Whales Are

> But what surface have we fallen through,
> Here beneath the trees? What do we see in our infinity
> if each is all the same, or all unknown?
> —*Molly Lou Freeman*

Halfway down an alder slope, through an opening in the jumble of branches and leaves, Craig's son Lars spots them. "Look, killer whales! They're coming into the bay!" Even though he's only eight, Lars knows whales from a mile away and five hundred feet up. Since he was six months old, he and his sisters have been bundled and stashed on his parents' research boats every summer. At Whale Camp, he rubbed holes in his baby socks bouncing on the wall tent's plywood floor, his Johnny Jump-Up suspended from the ridgepole. "Listen," he says, "you can even *hear* them. They're over *there*." He points; we squint. There, in ponds of sunlight, we see black fins, breath smoke.

"Good eyes, Lars," says Craig. "Let's go." We lurch down the mountainside, branches tearing at our hair and our faces.

On the beach, we gallop, digging wedges into sand with our rubber boots. In the distance, a few yards offshore, the first bubble-cloud rises, and we run for it. A fin slits shadows at the sea edge. When we get closer, we tiptoe. Five killer whales slide along shore, releasing air so they can sink. White bubble-rings bloom and phosphoresce on the water's surface. It's called beach-rubbing. On beaches with particular slopes and small, round pebbles, killer whales approach shore to slide their bodies along the bottom. One bay to the south, in the winter of 1918–19, the artist Rockwell Kent, holed up with his nine-year-old son at the homestead of Lars Olson, a seventy-one-year-old Swede, observed the phenomenon. Kent might have seen the mother of Aialik, the oldest female in this group, rubbing on his beach.

Craig and I, unthinking, pull off our boots and socks, make to unbutton our shirts and jeans, to jump into the water, where the whales are. Lars asks, "What are you guys doing?" and we look at each other and laugh. What *are* we doing? We fall heavily onto the beach, side by side and watch. The fifty yards separating the whales from us might as well be the Gulf of Alaska. We can't—and shouldn't—cross it.

Even though we've been studying killer whales for two decades, fishermen still don't quite understand what we do out here. They call us "whale watchers." They shake their heads at Craig, a fisherman himself for twenty years, who, instead of sleeping during closures, raced off in his seine skiff to find killer whales.

Listen, I want to say, we're not *tourists*. We're doing *research*.

But what we do is watch. We watch from shore, with our boots askew on the ground. We watch from the boat's deck, poised with our notebooks, pencils, cameras, binoculars, with vials in which we place samples of whale skin. The whales visit our dreams, where they watch us. So what should we be called—scientists, voyeurs, observers, natural historians, writers, intruders, watchers? The killer whales are called *aaxlu, takxukuak, agliuk, mesungesak, polossatik, skana, keet*, feared one, grampus, blackfish, orca, big-fin, fat-chopper. Whale killer. From the realm of the dead. *Orcinus orca*.

~

In grad school, listening to a lecture, I stare out the window and scribble along the margins of my notebook pages:

outside
birch fingers cast smoke
ribbons on snow

The professor chalks formulas on the board, flips on the overhead projector's light, casts a graph on the wall of the oxygen consumption of a marine mammal. *The language is like this*, I write in my notebook:

kinetic
isotope

extrapolate
index

The formula makes sense. Someone has figured this out, disproved an old theory about the way whales dive. I memorize the formula, stash it like some possibly useful thing into that catch-all drawer in my mind.

~

In another part of my mind, in a dream, I'm standing on the *Lucky Star*'s stern with Lars. In the boat's wake, a pod of beaked whales circles. They twist in the foam, their eyes glinting up. When Lars reaches out his hand, a whale grabs it and won't let go. Using all of my strength, I yank him free.

When I told a Yup'iq woman about this dream, she called it a warning. In her Bering Sea village, she was taught that killer whales must never be hunted or bothered, that we mustn't touch them.

But we want to know.

We want to know, like the raven, who, in a Chugachmiut Native legend, swims into a killer whale's mouth and finds an old woman sitting inside the whale. She asks, "How did you come here?" The raven answers, "I called him. I wanted to know what was inside him."

~

During my first summer out in Prince William Sound as a volunteer, running the *Whale 1*'s predecessor, a tiny, problematic skiff my field assistant and I finally—after countless breakdowns—dubbed "Dorky Orky," one of my tasks was to decide on a project for my master's thesis. Initially, I felt drawn to the quieter ways of humpback whales, who stayed in protected areas near Whale Camp to feed. But small groups of killer whales kept passing by camp, hugging the shoreline. They were AT1 transients, mammal-eaters about which little was known except that they were mostly silent and difficult to follow. But we did follow them, into and out of every bay and small passage in the southwestern Sound as they searched for harbor seals. Sometimes, anchored up in a tiny cove, we woke in darkness to their sharp exhalations around the boat. Other times, after following them for hours along shore, one of us peering over the bow to watch for bottom, the whales would veer into open water and attack Dall's porpoise pods, throwing the 400-pound black-and-white animals—resembling miniature killer whales—twenty feet into the air. My mantra became, "If we follow them long enough, we'll see something amazing." I grew curious about how those mostly silent whales communicated.

One day, my friend and I followed two AT1 transients from a small inflatable as they hunted harbor seals along an island shore. We lost them for several minutes, and then spotted silver mist above a rock. We let the boat drift near. Clinging tightly to the rock, its head craned back, eyes huge and black, a seal pup crouched above the waterline. A transient nudged the rock, but couldn't reach the seal, at least not yet; the tide was rising. Abruptly, the whale turned, joined the second whale, and swam rapidly across an open passage. We left the lucky seal and raced to catch the transients, but they'd vanished. Cutting the outboard in mid-passage so we might hear their blows, we stood up, scanning with binoculars.

I felt something through the bottom of my feet before I heard it. From the inflatable's wooden floorboards, a wail rose, and another, and another. My friend and I stared at each other.

"It's the whales. They must be right under us. Let's drop the hydrophone," I said.

I scrambled for the tape recorder, and we huddled over the small speaker adjusting knobs as long, descending, siren-like cries reverberated against underwater island walls. In the distance, other whales answered, faintly. I'd never heard transients call before. It was like a stone had sung. I knew then. I wanted to learn the language of the whales that were mostly silent.

In grad school, I learned the art of detachment, learned to watch how I said things, to listen for anthropomorphism, like applying the word *language* to non-humans. As scientists, we distinguish ourselves from whale huggers, lovers, groupies, and gurus, from those who think of whales as spiritual beings. We learn the evolutionary, biological basis for an animal's behavior. We study the various theories and counter-theories and debate their merits: reciprocal altruism, game theory, optimality theory, cost-benefit analysis. At scientific meetings, in animal behavior seminars, we don't debate whether animals have feelings. It's *terra incognita*. But on the research boat, or at the breakfast table before the meeting begins, some of us talk about these things. One non-scientist friend, puzzled by the ways of science, asked "Isn't it strange to assume that humans are the only creatures with feelings, that we are so different from other animals?" Is it "animapomorphic" to ascribe animal traits to humans? If it's wrong to suppose that animals might share qualities with humans, then how do we see ourselves? Alone at the tip of some renegade branch of the tree of life?

Out in the field, summer after summer, we search for knowledge, employing the scientific method: observation, hypothesis, data collection, analysis, discussion, conclusion. Poet and biologist Forrest Gander says that this method "has endured as a scientific model, and a very successful one, for it predicts that when we do something, we will obtain certain results. But if we approach with a different model, we will ask different questions." To create a new model: that prospect challenges all of the questions I've learned to ask—and not to ask.

Over the course of a four-month-long field season, sometimes we see killer whales every day, and sometimes weeks go by without them. Often, we've spotted distant whales, come near them to take photographs, and they've vanished. Other days, we've followed killer whales for twenty-four hours. Then, after so long, even the observing eye becomes insufficient, so we listen. In darkness, we navigate by the sound of their breathing.

We take turns sleeping. I'm leaning on the boat's dashboard, echo of engine roar dying, wave slaps against the boat's hull taking over. I drop the hydrophone down to listen. Two in the morning, just past summer solstice, Montague Strait is dimly lit, but it's too dark to see the whales. I don't hear anything. They're down for a long dive, or we've lost them. I hold my breath. Then, a few hundred yards away,

whoosh-ah   whoosh   whoosh whoosh-ah

I stare in the direction of the sound, hear water closing around it.

Another summer. For eleven days, Molly Lou and I search hundreds of miles without finding killer whales. On the twelfth day, we hear radio reports of a large group forty miles from camp, in open water. After roaring past Smith Island and Little Smith Island at twenty knots, we drop the hydrophone, climb onto the cabin top, scan with binoculars, radio the boats who reported the whales. The water's still. No one responds. On the hydrophone, waves lap, lap, lap.

After searching an hour, we give up, then devise a plan. No more running around wasting fuel. We're going to wait, let the whales come to us. We return to camp, and the next morning we gather paper and books, food and a thermos. We run the boat a mile off camp, out in the passage, and shut down. After dropping the hydrophone and scanning around, putting out a radio call, we settle into the boat, build a fire in the tiny stove. Every half hour, one of us pulls on raingear and climbs onto the roof to scan with binoculars.

A couple of hours pass this way. I look at my watch, put down my book. It's my turn to scan. I glance out as I reach for my jacket. Fins rise around the boat.

It worked! I shout, and we rush to put on raingear, gather cameras. The rest of the day, we follow the whales.

The same trick never works again. We're constantly second-guessing. Should we sit still? We call that the "sit and wait" hypothesis. Should we move? We call that the "Lance and Kathy" method, after colleagues who averaged a hundred miles a day one summer. Once, Craig and I searched the outer coast of Montague Island, over seventy miles, and saw nothing. Our friend radioed that killer whales were off Point Helen, a few miles from Whale Camp, and only about ten miles from us, as a raven would fly.

If we could have, like the lunatic film character Fitzcaraldo, drug our boat over that mountain, we'd have been there.

That night, we watched a wildlife DVD about a group of filmmakers who spent four years trying to photograph snow leopards in the Indian Himalaya. They never saw a kill, never saw a litter of cubs, their two greatest desires. They didn't see snow leopards for the first several weeks, just tracks and scat. They concentrated on these tidbits, mapping them until they sensed patterns. Even after decades in the field, we constantly have to revamp our intentions and strategies, remind ourselves to concentrate, not on our desires, not on the past, but on clues, which is hard when you're lifting fluke-prints off water.

The morning after we watched the film, three AT1 transients slid past our anchorage. We heard them first on the hydrophone. They were hunting marine mammals offshore, diving for ten minutes at a time, constantly changing direction. The north wind blew up. We lost them after an hour. We managed to take one identification photo.

In the Tlingit language, the word for killer whale, *keet*, means "supernatural being." We'll never know its true connotation, but it fits. In nature, creatures defy our assumptions. In the 1980s, biologists divided fish-eating killer whales into pods, extended family groups that remained together for life. Recently, that story has been revised. These societies orbit around the matriline, mothers and offspring. Pods can fracture. The loss of a key female may cause a family to rupture, for bonds to loosen. Discoveries reveal the *keet* nature of the wild animal. And the more we know, the longer we stay, the more we care, and caring, like anthropomorphism, is tricky ground for that detached creature, the scientist.

For the past few years, we've been collecting samples from killer whales to measure contaminant levels in their blubber, to extract DNA from their skin. We've learned that their populations are small, a few hundred animals, so an oil spill or a die-off of salmon or seals can be catastrophic. We've confirmed that residents and transients don't interbreed, though they share the same waters, that transients carry high PCB and DDT levels in their blubber, that mothers pass these poisons to calves through their milk. But to learn this, we have to approach whales more closely than we do to take photographs. To do this, we point a rifle at a whale and shoot a biopsy dart into its body. The dart pops out after snagging an inch-long piece of flesh on its thread-like barb, and we scoop it from the water with a dip net. To do this, Craig and I argue through our conflicted feelings. *We can't dart now; they're resting. These animals are rare. We can't dart in front of tour boats. We might not have another chance. We've probably darted enough animals in this group. We need more samples for the statistical tests. We have to have a common mind. I hate all this.*

Even Lars, who's enthusiastic about shooting, scrunches down in the bow, fingers plugged in his ears, eyes shut tight when the shot's fired.

From the boat's cabin top, I scanned Montague Strait in light diffused by high clouds, looking for blows. I spotted a white glittering, then another. It was the kind of haze made by a leaping whale when its body collapsed onto the water.

We raced that way and found killer whales, took identification pictures of their dorsal fins and flanks, recognized them as Gulf of Alaska transients. The last time I'd seen them was four years before. They'd never been biopsied, but we knew that their calls differed from those of the local AT1 transients, so they might be from a completely separate population. That day, Craig wasn't there to wield the dart gun, and my field assistant—my husband, John—and I had to do it ourselves.

For the next two hours, the whales led us past Danger Island, into the Gulf. John, more comfortable with a rifle than I was from his years in the Alaskan bush, shot three times without success. Out of Montague Strait's strong current, the water calmed to a swell. In my impatience, I took the gun. John pulled the boat in close to the whales, and I sighted on an old female's scarred saddle patch. Without thinking, I pulled the trigger. The dart hit the saddle patch and bounced out. She slapped her tail and dove.

"We got a sample," I shouted, elated, when I pulled up the dart and saw blubber protruding from the tip. I gave John the gun on the next approach, and he darted another female.

"We're getting pretty far out here," he said after I wrapped the third sample in foil and stored it in the cooler. "I think we should go back." I glanced toward the Sound. We were at least four miles from shore now, and the whales were heading steadily south in the direction of Hawaii. As we drifted, we watched them disappear.

An hour later, anchored up at Foxfarm Bay, just inside Cape Elrington, intent on processing samples and thrilled at our success, I didn't notice John watching me.

"I've never seen you that way before," he said.

"What way?" I asked, looking up.

"You were so angry and impatient, even rude at times, and then, suddenly, when you got what you wanted, you were ecstatic. A real Dr. Jekyll/Mr. Hyde thing. It was scary."

I stared across the bay, where a sea otter lazily rolled and dove and brought up some kind of shellfish. Inside me, a nauseous feeling rose.

―

I haven't darted many killer whales since. It's Craig who wields the gun. And there are whales we've never been able to dart, mostly sea lion hunters with torn fins. They sometimes approach our boat, curious, staring at us with inscrutable eyes. Once, a female grazed her body along the skiff's side, her mouth open, showing rows of perfect teeth. "What are you saying?" I called after her as she swam away.

Years ago, another whale drifted under the bow where I stood, looking down. She held a harbor seal in her jaws. Blood from the seal's body throbbed.

Science trains me to be detached in moments like those, but sometimes I'm angry or panicked in the field, when I can't get what I want, what I *must* have. When I face the fact that I have no control over what's invisible, what binds me so viscerally to my desires, what decides when the whales will find me.

―

After several days without whales in Resurrection Bay, Craig and I overhear a radio conversation between tour boats. Killer whales are traveling along the rocky shoreline of Fox Island, fifteen miles from where we're floating, our hydrophone down. They're heading for the cape, out of the Bay and out to sea. The skippers think they're transients—the ones they call "the bad boys"—two large AT1 males that hunt harbor seals in ice floes off the Aialik Glacier.

We drop our books and scramble to start the engine, call a skipper, get a location and direction of travel, and roar across the Bay, coaxing as much speed as we can out of the *Whale 2*. When we spot the whales, we know right away they're not the local "bad boys." Their fins are too broad and tall. As I slide the boat in parallel to the whales so we can take pictures, I scan photos of transient dorsal fins in the killer whale catalog.

"Who do you think they are?" Craig asks, clicking off frames. "They're awfully tolerant for Gulf of Alaska transients."

The whales travel slowly, breathing for eight breaths, then diving for ten minutes. They follow a regular compass heading east, directly past Cape Resurrection, toward the Sound. I stare at two blurry photos, then back up at the whales.

"They *are* Gulf of Alaska transients. They're the AT30s." The pictures are poor, taken during a single encounter seven years ago in bad weather.

We spend the next hour trying to get biopsy samples. Tour boats come to watch them, so we don't dart. Darts miss. Once, a dart pops out of a whale but doesn't take a sample. Another time, we're too far away when they surface. Other times, they change direction slightly when they dive. I plead to them, to Craig's amusement, as I position the boat. "Whales, please let us take these tiny samples. We'll never have to do this again. It's for your own good!"

We call out names for them, Chubby Rain and Heavy Rain. Despite our blundering, our absurd behavior, the whales let us approach closely again and again, and finally we have some samples.

Floating off Killer Bay, we watch them disappear. "Don't you wish you knew where they were going?" Craig asks. "Someday, with a little transmitter attached to them, we won't have to wonder where they are."

Now I can barely make out two distant black triangles among rolling hills of water, and I think of them unwatched by anyone for eight more years. They're swimming off the edge of the known world, like hapless ships on ancient charts. They might dive right through the sea realm, resurface in some other, a realm of the supernatural. A young Sugpiaq man from Nanwalek, a tiny village in outer Cook Inlet, told me there's a lake near his home that's bottomless. A killer whale jumped into that lake, he said, dove to the bottom, pushed through and emerged in another lake.

We cling to what we know. In response to Descartes' mechanistic view of the universe, Blaise Pascal said, "The silence of these infinite spaces terrifies me."

Science. It seems solid, but it's mostly space, like a gill net I drop over the world. Two transients pass through its web, leave me holding a tiny sample, a pencil.

A young scientist seeks mentors. Bud Fay, my major professor in grad school, an expert on the walrus, showed me how a scientist could learn from and gain the respect of Native people. Hunters on St. Lawrence Island still remember him. Craig, other whale biologists, and those I know through their discoveries, their tenacity, their eyes that see and ears that hear what others miss, are my biologist heroes. I met Mike, my last mentor, one afternoon at Chenega Village. He rode his four-wheeler down the steep ramp to the dock. In the vibrating silence after he'd shut down the engine, he sat and watched me as I pumped fuel onto the *Whale 1*. His look was inscrutable. There was no smile. Under his cap, his eyes were shadowed. He could have been angry. Non-Natives were not always welcomed in the village. I tensed when he climbed off the four-wheeler and, hands in pockets, strolled over to the boat. "Seen any whales?" he asked, grinning.

He was all sinew, brown skin, black hair, and a small, bowlegged frame. He wore a plaid wool shirt, stiff new dungarees, and wire-framed glasses. I knew he was considered a village elder, although I couldn't tell his age. He coughed often, into his fist, turning his head away. I introduced myself, but afterward, he'd show up at the dock whenever I was there and greet me, "Hey, *Whale 1*."

He dropped bits of knowledge into our conversations, where he'd seen whales, how seals in the area were declining. I knew he hunted seals and fished for salmon but learned only from other villagers that he was one of the most respected elders in the Sound and one of the last seal hunters in his village. I also learned he was dying of lung cancer. He'd gained his knowledge by roaming the Sound in a boat in all seasons, watching. Since the oil spill, he'd assisted biologists on their projects—on octopus, harbor seals, subsistence traditions—and strove to involve his village in the science.

I began to look for Mike when I came to Chenega, wandering to his house, inviting myself in for a cup of tea. Somehow, I felt attached to him. Our conversations were brief. But, after time, when he saw me, he hugged me. He teased me. When I told him what I wanted to be, he shook his head. "Why do you need to do that? You don't need to go to school to do that. You just need to live out here."

The smell of burning alder drifts up from Mike's smokehouse. He's gone today. He's hunting seals.

Molly Lou and I anchor the boat in front of camp. It's sunny, but the wind's come up, so we decide to take turns trying on the dry suit, snorkel, and mask and swimming through the eelgrass and kelp beds. Molly Lou helps me with the zipper.

> *I put on*
> *the body armor of black rubber*
> *the absurd flippers*
> *the grave and awkward mask.*

I hear words from Adrienne Rich's poem in my head when I drop feet-first from the boat's side into the sea.

*There is no one
to tell me when the ocean
will begin.*

After I pull the black rubber away from my neck to release air, the dry suit clings to my body like loose skin. I place my face in the water and breathe through the snorkel, wheezing rapidly at first out of fear, and the sound is loud, like the breaths of someone dying.

Eelgrass and kelp stream below me. Now my breathing sounds as if someone is breathing for me. I paddle. I make arcs through the water with my hands. Tiny sculpins wink in and out of battered fronds. As I swim along a rock outcrop, I look for seals. I glide along rocks and quiet my movements, searching the sandy bottom. My body blots out the light above me. I'm hungry. I search the whole island's submerged perimeter.

At times like these, I get closer to the water.

⁓

A friend of mine kayaking in the Sound met Mike once and asked him if he knew me. Mike chuckled, said, "I hear her on the radio . . . She's wondering where the whales are."

Mike died four winters ago. The last time I saw him, he had to breathe from an oxygen bottle.

⁓

According to traditional stories from all along Alaska's coastline, when killer whales come into a bay, someone will die. A Sugpiaq woman from Nanwalek told me why. "When killer whales come near the village, they're calling someone to join them, so we're sad. A week or two later, someone dies."

There's a killer whale we've named Jack, after the late Jack Evanoff of Chenega Village. His niece, Mary, told me that when Jack was an old man, "He always said he'd come back as a killer whale with a partially bent over dorsal fin." People told her that they'd seen such a whale out in the Sound. It's true. There's only one. He's a salmon-hunter from a pod that centers its range in Prince William Sound. His fin curls to starboard, and from the back it looks like a question mark. Lars calls him "Captain Hook."

Sometimes, anchored up in a storm in a place called Pony Cove, I joke with Lars about killer whales, make up crazy stories about what they do. I tell him an old tale:

Long ago, a man from Nanwalek followed some killer whales in his kayak. He thought they might lead him to seals. The whales dove at the head of a bay and disappeared. When the man paddled to shore, he saw human footprints leading into a cave. He followed them. Inside, he saw humans putting on killer whale skins. Once, I tell Lars, humans and animals spoke the same language.

Can science teach me this language?

Science teaches me that there's a truth somewhere, that I can find it, that I can listen and hear something. For years, I recorded the sounds of transients. I scrutinized each call on a sonograph analyzer. I scribbled descriptions of everything I saw. I identified hunting calls, resting calls, social calls, long-distance contact calls, but I never deciphered the language of the whale that eats only mammals, that speaks mostly silence. The language of the killer whale eluded me.

What I did learn was that it's not difficult, in the moment, to surrender to not knowing. To be a watcher. Like a transient, who finds its prey by listening, to be silent.

Once I found a picture of Mike as a child on the schoolhouse steps at Old Chenega. I recognized him by his big ears. Sometimes, Mike walked with me along the shore of his island. He'd stop suddenly, motion me to be quiet. "Listen," he'd say. "I hear something."

Montague Island's reflection extends a long way down into the water in the afternoon's heavy light. Whales swim along its snowy flanks, across green slopes, skim the tops of conifer stands, along bare rock, then dive down *into* the mountains. When they rise again, they break apart the island's reflection.

Lars drops a stone into the water. We watch it. The deeper we go, the more knowledge resembles a question mark. Who's asking the questions? We listen. We watch the stone sinking. We watch it spiral out of sight. Science. It's like that.

The Author Speaks!

This is the first essay I wrote that directly addressed the questions I have about science and being a scientist. I'd spent five years in graduate school, and even though I loved being out in Prince William Sound studying whales, I felt uneasy about Science (with a big "S," Science as a world view). I felt constricted by its rules, but, at the same time, I knew how valuable science was as way of discovering things about the world. I wrote "Wondering Where the Whales Are" as a way to come to peace about my role in the world of science, and as a way to honor my dear friend Mike Eleshansky, who died of lung cancer not long before I wrote the essay. I believe essays (like scientific studies) raise more questions than they answer. I raised as many questions as I could in the essay, with the hope that readers would come to their own conclusions. I believe that the best way of knowing the world is through as many lenses as possible: science, art, philosophy, traditional knowledge, direct observation, spirituality, physics, literature, experience. An ideal education, in my mind, would approach each subject from as many angles as possible. When I write about killer whales, that's what I try to do.

After you read this essay, think about the ways you know the world. Pick something you know a little about: a car engine, trees, a skateboard, weather, math, American history, friendship, clouds, health, politics, etc. What are all the ways you've learned about this, starting with your earliest memories? Who are your teachers, inside and outside school? As a class, pick one thing, clouds, for example. Brainstorm everything you know, as a group. What is your collective knowledge about this thing, and where did your knowledge come from? What have you taught someone else?

Questions:
1. Think about the epigraph that opens "Wondering Where the Whales Are." It poses two questions. How do they relate to the essay? Which words in the epigraph link most strongly to the ideas presented in the essay? If there was one question this essay was asking, what would it be?

2. What scientific information is passed on in this essay? What questions does the writer have about science?
3. In the essay's opening scene, the writer and Craig start taking off their shoes, as though they were going to jump into the ocean with the whales. Lars asks, "What are you guys doing?" What *are* they doing? And why do they stop?
4. Besides the scientific way, what different ways of knowing things about the world, or about killer whales specifically, are proposed in the essay?
5. What's the relationship, in the writer's mind, between traditional Native knowledge of killer whales and modern scientific knowledge? What does Saulitis learn from Mike?
6. What does the writer mean by the term "animopomorphic?"
7. Explain the writer's reaction to darting the killer whales, when she says, "Inside me, a nauseous feeling rises." Why does she feel nauseous? And what does he mean when John says she's a real "Dr. Jekyll/Mr. Hyde?"
8. Why are scientists supposed to be "detached"?
9. In the essay, emphasis is placed on the way things are named. Discuss different examples of names given to killer whales (or people, or places) in the essay. Why are names important? What happens when you name a wild animal?
10. Explain the "net" metaphor for science. How is science, in the essay, like a "giant net"? What are the holes? What are the threads? What are the knots? What is the net used for? What's captured in the net? What escapes?
11. When the writer puts on a drysuit and snorkels along the island shore, what's she searching for? Why, in the next very short section, does she say "Sometimes it seems I'm getting closer to the water"?
12. Why is this essay broken up into such short sections? How does the way the essay's put together relate to what the essay says?
13. Explain the final image and statement of the essay: the stone falling through the water. And the last sentence: "Science. It's like that."
14. Non-fiction writers choose what and whom to leave out of essays. Each "character" in an essay is there for a reason. What is Lars's role in the essay? Why is he included?

15. Why does the writer make a point of mentioning Mike's big ears near the end of the essay?

Maurya Simon

Black Widow

This dangler who visits me
disguised as agile beauty
is death's sweet marionette,
an eight-legged, swollen speck—
a tiny, black forget-me-not
spinning her soundless tune
with a luminescent thread.

Her husband taps out a code
of courtship quite cautiously
as he slowly tightropes nearer:
pheromones prescribe his destiny,
yet he seems a wayward star
moving to collide into the sun,
imploding to unfurl
a million filaments of light.

I watch their dance tonight
and see extend through history
the sacrificial slant some lives
slide down upon—star, spider, man—
each body bright, marked for life
by an invisible hourglass that's
tipped, emptying its sand.

The Author Speaks!

This is a poem about time and mortality and sacrifice. After watching a black widow spider one day, having recovered from my initial fear, I began to think about what people (and stars) have in common with these dangerous critters, namely a limited life span, and the possibility of making sacrifices as part of our nature and circumstances.

Miriam Sagan

Take a Left At My Mailbox

Cross Sierra Vista and enter the cul-de-sac
Where the pavement ends
Cross over and down into the acequia full of trash
Where a sodden quilt lies in the middle of where
Stream once moved sand
In eddies. The homeless camp
Disintegrates, only one mattress left
And I'm lecturing my daughter
Who steps back to photograph it
"Don't come here alone,"
And she retorts: "I have since I was eight," and then
"It's so peaceful here, but
I hate the fence."
This is no arroyo, cut by rain
But a remnant of man, an irrigation ditch
Now watering detritus, the leftover, cast off, plastic bags, and worse.
From here you can cut
Up behind the Indian School
Past the transformer I didn't even know was there
And come out where there once were tracks
Now just the runners half-buried in soil.
It's Baca Street! We're back
In the neighborhood where my daughter
Immediately becomes lost

"I don't get straight streets," she says.
My money's good here, I buy two cups of foamy chai
And look in her face, turning from girl to woman
And want to construct
My map of the lost.

The Author Speaks!

This is the title poem of my book *Map of the Lost* (University of New Mexico Press, 2008). It was inspired by the desire to make a literal map, directions the reader could follow, of part of my hometown of Santa Fe, New Mexico. What is "lost" is a series of places due to urban change, but, also, the poems are about my daughter growing up and leaving home. Of course, each poem is an attempt to preserve something that is changing—maybe futile, but necessary.

Peggy Shumaker

In Praise, Ephemera

At dawn feeding swans, upended
by the ice shelf, black beaks
champing half-thawed weeds,

draw us to the riverbank. Grizzled feathers,
echo of boots over rotting snow.   Far between,
few, tundra swans step out on late ice.

Glacial melt, snow melt
hustle downstream—
ice dams hold tight

jostled swathes of half-lace ice.
Knife-edged narrow
leads open, sliced river swollen.

Muskrat and beaver gnaw
new shoots of red willow,
open winter lodges. Fresh water, air.

Pollen, lavish, carpets the
quick and the dead, blessing the
revived, blessing the remade.

Season of cold broken. Season of ice broken. Season of
tattered shirtsleeves. Bare hands
useful again after burrowing all winter.

Voles gather first shoots of new grasses,
weave fresh sheaves to put by, chew new roots, shoots, and
xylem, drunk on the season's sugars risen

yesterday and today, this hour
zipping by, lifting off, wild swan in clear sky.

The Author Speaks!

I live on the banks of the Chena River in Fairbanks, Alaska. This poem takes place during breakup, when after seven months of hard winter the river ice begins to crack and move downstream. (This usually happens in late April or in May.)

The poem looks at what can't last—the presence of swans, birds that stop by for one morning before moving on to their brooding ponds further north. It looks at the warm season promised by the melt, all too short in Interior Alaska. This poem praises the great energy awakened in the new season.

Students might enjoy writing their own poem in praise of what doesn't last—what cannot last. So much in our lives can't last. We have to savor what's only here for a moment.

Students might also enjoy trying the almost-invisible form I used in this poem. Did you notice? If you look at the first letter of each line, the poem uses the whole alphabet. This is called an abecedarium.

Steven Schutzman

Five More Minutes

Time: *Early evening.*

Setting: *A front porch with porch swing or glider.*

Characters:
LAURA – mid 20s
GREGORY – mid 20s

LAURA *inert on porch swing, staring toward* AUDIENCE. GREGORY *enters, home from work.*

Gregory
   Laura? (*Beat*) Laura? (*Beat*) You okay? (*Beat*)

Laura
   Oh, hi Gregory.

Gregory
   I...

Laura
   You want to sit down?

Gregory
   No thanks. Are you all right?

LAURA

I don't have the energy to make this swing swing.

GREGORY

You want a push or something?

LAURA

I kept thinking I'll stay here five more minutes. Just five more minutes. Five more minutes. And now the whole day's gone.

GREGORY

Yeah, I saw you out here when I left for work this morning.

LAURA

Nine straight hours.

GREGORY

In your bathrobe with the flowers.

LAURA

I got up to change because the stupid window guy was supposed to come but he didn't show up. And to go to the bathroom.

GREGORY

I'm sorry you're feeling bad.

LAURA

I don't have the energy to feel bad.

Gregory

Anyway, I hate to add to your problems but I'm moving out. I'm giving notice. End of the month. Okay?

Laura

Fine. (*Beat. Beat.*) So that's it after three years?

Gregory

He slashed my tires.

Laura

I understand.

Gregory

I had to take the bus to work.

Laura

I'm sorry.

Gregory

I know he's your boyfriend but the guy's a lowlife with the foulest mouth in the world. You heard what he said about me.

Laura

You sniveling pansy Jewish bookworm.

Gregory

Real loud. So the whole neighborhood could hear.

Laura

You're not Jewish.

GREGORY

That's not the point. In his primitive mind, he sees someone with a book, he tries to run them over.

LAURA

Because you left a note on his truck.

GREGORY

To ask him not to park it so it blocks my car.

LAURA

He doesn't like being left notes.

GREGORY

Obviously.

LAURA

He likes to talk man to man.

GREGORY

So you're taking his side?

LAURA

No. Just saying.

GREGORY

The guy's a total maniac.

LAURA

In case you want to reconsider, I kicked him out last night.

GREGORY

Oh. Really?

LAURA

And I really don't have the energy to find a new tenant.

GREGORY

Gee, thanks a lot.

LAURA

No, I'll miss you. (*Beat*) You know what I'm going to do: Just sit here and let my cats have litter after litter. Soon the house will crumble and be overrun by cats and I'll be a very strange lady.

GREGORY

Maybe you're depressed.

LAURA

I don't have the energy to be depressed.

Scene grows inert. Pause.

GREGORY

Anyway, he'll be back.

LAURA

Yeah. Maybe. I'm not real good at the alone thing like you are.

GREGORY

That's not something a person's good at. It's something that happens to them.

LAURA

So you're not good at it?

GREGORY

No.

LAURA

Too bad. Because I was going to ask you your secret.

GREGORY

Well, maybe, I have gotten a little good at it.

LAURA

It's all right. What's the point?

Scene inert. Pause.

GREGORY

So that's it? Because you're not good at being alone, you're going to take him back?

LAURA

I feel like a vegetable. Like I don't want to move ever again. And so it was five more minutes, five more minutes. Five minutes put a limit on it but then I changed my mind about moving each time and wound up staying here all day.

GREGORY

I think you're depressed.

LAURA

And I'm not a vegetable that's growing either. I don't have enough energy to actually grow. Maybe if I sit here long enough some stranger will see me and have me taken away. Because there's no one who cares enough to actually call anyone.

GREGORY

You want me to call someone?

LAURA

There's no one to call.

GREGORY

Oh.

LAURA

If a person does any one thing long enough, even the most normal thing, like sitting on the porch swing or saying hello or sharpening pencils, if it just goes on and on, hello, hello, hello, hello, or non-stop sharpening, it becomes abnormal.

GREGORY

Well, yeah. Like the guy sitting on the bench at the bus stop this morning, just sitting, just staring. He seemed okay, regular, because staring is what guys do on benches early before work in the morning but he didn't get on the bus and there he was staring like that when I got off this afternoon.

LAURA

All day like me.

Gregory

Yeah and he was dressed perfectly regular but then you figure he doesn't have a job or maybe anywhere to go to.

Laura

I don't have a job either.

Gregory

You figure, that's probably the guy's regular bench.

Laura

I quit the flower shop. Remember it? You came in once?

Gregory

I didn't have anyone to buy flowers for. I just spotted you in there. I remember you told me how much you loved flowers.

Laura

Flowers.

Gregory

Yeah and you told me why you loved them so much.

Laura

Flowers have no use.

Gregory

Uh, right.

LAURA

No practical use. They're useless. That's the beauty of flowers, just to sit there and be beautiful.

LAURA *chokes up.*

GREGORY

Is there anything I can do?

LAURA *shakes her head No. Scene inert. Pause.*

GREGORY (CONT'D)

Or, or, get this, maybe the guy had a job to go to, or did have one, who knows? Because I never took the bus before. So what I saw this morning was the morning the guy decided to turn from a regular guy into an irregular guy.

LAURA

You don't decide that. It's another thing that happens to you.

GREGORY

Right. Right. But maybe just then was when he snapped. Because in this city you don't know what regular looking person might snap right where you are. Because people here are snapping all over the place.

LAURA

Like me.

GREGORY

Snap, snap, snap.

LAURA

I'm just another snapper.

GREGORY

Ha! (*Beat*) Sorry. It just sounded funny.

LAURA

Heh.

Scene inert. Pause.

GREGORY

When I first moved in here you were real different, before you hooked up with him and he sapped your strength.

LAURA

Yeah?

GREGORY

Yeah. Like, you know, different. Special.

LAURA

But then my parents died in the car accident.

GREGORY

You're still real sad over it, huh?

LAURA

I don't know. Numb. But they left me this house so all I have to do is sit here and collect rent on the units.

GREGORY

And take care of the place.

LAURA

Well, he does that. Did that.

GREGORY

You're going to let him come back, aren't you?

LAURA

I don't know. It's the alone thing. How do you do it, Gregory really? I wish I could. Maybe you could teach me like you almost taught me to juggle that time.

GREGORY

Until the maniac threatened to beat the crap out of me for standing behind you and touching your wrists. What a lowlife.

LAURA

Yeah.

GREGORY

You liked that?

LAURA

Well, he was jealous. He's not really a very demonstrative person ever.

GREGORY

Try leaving him a note. Come on, smile, just a little.

Laura

Heh. Heh.

Scene inert. Pause.

Gregory

You really want to know how I do the alone thing?

Laura

Yeah. Why not?

Gregory

See, there was this Senator in ancient Rome . . .

Laura

What?

Gregory

Listen. There was this Senator in ancient Rome who knew that one day some political enemy was sure to poison him in the Senate where they were always having like libations with wine, so he took small doses of the poison to build up his resistance.

Laura

So you're building up resistance to being alone by being alone.

Gregory

Something like that. Yeah. Maybe.

Laura

That's dumb, Gregory.

Gregory

No, it's stoicism. Like the Romans. We're all ultimately alone.

Laura

Hard to find anyone, isn't it?

Gregory

Yeah, because the odds in this city are terrible. I hate this place. I don't know anybody but I feel like I already know everybody.

Laura

That sucks.

Gregory

I move here after college, good job, nothing happens to me, and five minutes later three years have passed.

Laura

That's a funny way to put it.

Gregory

I didn't just make it up. I've said it a lot of times before.

Laura

You didn't have to tell me that.

Gregory

Yeah, well, right, but, in case I ever do meet anyone, the story about the Senator is a good story, besides me being overworked, wouldn't you say, as a woman, to explain my, you know, almost non-existent relationship history?

Laura

No. Too whiny.

Gregory

Whiny? It's stoicism.

Laura

I don't care. It's whiny. Try telling her you were waiting for the right person to come along.

Gregory

Stoicism is the opposite of whiny. Stoics believe that, since everything is the result of divine will, a person should calmly accept whatever happens to him without passion, joy or pain.

Laura

Calmly. Like a vegetable. We're two vegetables. We're two of a kind. You sure you don't want to sit down?

Gregory

No. I better not.

Scene inert. Pause.

Laura

Anyway, your Senator story sounds like one of the excuses for not doing anything losers are always coming up with.

Gregory

Yeah? Really?

LAURA

Has it ever worked with a woman?

GREGORY

I only just read about it last night.

LAURA

You were reading about ancient Rome last night?

GREGORY

Yeah, after your maniac boyfriend tried to run me over.

LAURA

You were actually reading about ancient Rome, Gregory, like in your free time. I think that is so cool.

GREGORY

But you're more attracted to lowlifes who work on their trucks all day.

LAURA

Not really.

GREGORY

And mooch out on the rent.

LAURA

He wouldn't stay if he had to pay anything.

GREGORY

Now that must make you feel great.

Laura

It makes me feel like a vegetable.

Gregory

You're selling yourself short, Laura.

Laura

I'm a string bean with low self-esteem.

Gregory

That's funny. Maybe you're feeling a little better now, huh?

Laura

My parents die, I'm miserable, I hook up with him, get used to him and dependent on him, get made miserable by him and now I can't get rid of him. I'm like addicted to misery.

Gregory

See? You're just like the Senator in the story, taking little doses of poison and that maniac's the poison.

Laura

Right.

Gregory

But for what?

Laura

I don't know.

Gregory

Maybe you're taking all these little heartbreaks to protect yourself from a big heartbreak.

Laura

What big heartbreak is that, Gregory?

Gregory

I don't know. One of the big heartbreaks.

Laura

He couldn't break my heart because it was already broken. All he can do is step on the pieces.

Gregory

Well, don't let him.

Laura

I can't help it.

Gregory

You love him? Still?

Laura

No. I hate myself.

Gregory

Oh. Yeah.

Laura

That's better?

Gregory

Uh, no.

Laura

So I snapped. Five more minutes. Five more minutes. Snapping's a good word for it because I can't connect with me, the me I used to know, who, who . . . I don't know . . . who liked arranging flowers, who wanted to learn to juggle.

Gregory

I could still teach you. Come on. Let's do it. Up we go.

Laura

Forget it. I don't have the energy.

Scene inert. Pause.

Gregory

There's a second part to the Roman Senator story I read. One day, he heard his enemies were coming to his house to kill him, which in ancient Rome meant getting your skin raked off with these razor sharp rakes and then being drawn and quartered with ropes pulled by horses, so he takes a massive dose of the poison to commit suicide, but guess what? His plan works, the poison doesn't kill him and he has to endure this horrible torture, raked and drawn and quartered before he dies.

Laura

Wow.

GREGORY

Yeah. Great story, huh? He takes poison his whole life to protect himself and then winds up tortured because of it. His plan backfired big time. That's, you know, I learned it in college, literary term . . . ironic. That's irony.

LAURA

Right. I could never keep irony straight. Define irony, it'd say on the final and I'd start to feel sick to my stomach.

GREGORY

Because that Senator thought he was protecting himself but he was really endangering himself.

LAURA

Right. Like me with my boyfriend, former boyfriend.

GREGORY

Because the Senator thought he was avoiding pain but he was really setting himself up for more pain.

LAURA

Right. Like me.

GREGORY

Because what you think is happening is not what's really happening. That's irony.

LAURA

I wish I had that test in front of me right now.

Gregory

Define irony.

Laura

Move in with me.

Gregory

What?

Laura

Move in with me. That's irony. Because you think you're moving out but you're really moving in.

Gregory

A plus.

Laura

No, I mean it.

Gregory

You mean it?

Laura

Yeah, I do. I want you to move in with me. I've always liked you. And see how we can talk. We've been talking longer now than I ever talked with him in my life. Somehow talking with you is very soothing to me. You're much better for me than he is, so why not?

Gregory

But it's running away from pain again . . . from heartbreak . . . on the rebound . . . and here I am . . . so you don't have to be alone . . . it's just probably the opposite of what you should do.

Laura

Right. It's ironic, I think.

Gregory

Okay, I'll do it. When?

Laura

Right now.

Gregory

What about him?

Laura

I'll put his stuff out on the curb.

Gregory

You will?

Laura

I'll call the cops, if he shows up.

Gregory

Okay, Sweetie. Move over.

GREGORY *sits and puts his arm around* LAURA. *She puts her head on his shoulder and they start swinging for the first time. Long pause.*

Gregory

You want me to teach you to juggle now.

Laura

No. I just want to sit here like this with you.

Gregory

You want to talk?

Laura

No. Let's be quiet.

Pause. Slight swinging.

Gregory

I never heard of this before.

Laura

What?

Gregory

Of people hooking up the way we just did.

Laura

So what?

Gregory

I feel like a vegetable.

Laura

I told you we're two of a kind. String bean.

Gregory

Cabbage.

They kiss. Scene inert.

Gregory (Cont'd)

This is funny. (*Beat*) Wait a minute. He's going to kill me.

Laura

No, he's gone for good.

Gregory

But . . .

Laura

I'll get the locks changed.

Gregory

I'm like that Senator. I'm going to be drawn and quartered by a broken down truck.

Laura

No you're not, silly.

Gregory

Let's go in.

Laura

No. Just five more minutes, okay?

Gregory
Okay.

They swing slightly. Scene becomes inert. Fade to black. End of play.

The Author Speaks!

Questions:
1. What kind of guy is Gregory? List some of his most striking character traits. What does Laura find charming about him?
2. What is Gregory trying to do in the first part of the play?
3. What is Laura like as a person? List some of her most striking character traits. Why might Gregory be attracted to her?
4. What does Laura want? Was it surprising or inevitable or both that she asked Gregory to move in with her?
5. Describe Laura and Gregory's past relationship and the nature of their interaction in the play.
6. Is the climax of the play believable? Explain why or why not.
7. Do Laura and Gregory have a good chance to make it as a couple? Explain why or why not.
8. Did you find it odd for them to hook up like this? Explain why or why not.
9. Explain the significance of the play's title.

Rex Wilder

Three Boomerangs

Crow

Crow!
Crushed under my tires.
And *now* I
slow . . .

Drops

Drops
of rain lay out their yoga
mats—and my pain
stops.

Found

Found:
Home from the beach, an argument
we thought the surf
had drowned.

The Author Speaks!

Ever tried to throw a boomerang? It's easy. Ever tried to make it come back, which is the whole point of a boomerang? Not so easy. I'd suggest you try to *write* one instead. The boomerang, as a poetic form, will give you the same satisfaction, not to mention *safely* impress your friends and teachers.

The rules are pretty straightforward. I should know; I made them. The first word (or syllable sometimes) must rhyme with the last word (or syllable). In other words, this elfish verse basically ends where it begins, something that feels absolutely amazing to the human ear. Try it, you'll see.

The boomerang also appeals to our visual senses, as it shape mimics the toy's breathtaking flight. The first line is usually just one word. I would suggest you make it an important word (not an "a" or a "the")—perhaps an exclamation *(Help!)*, or somebody's pet name *(Cupcake)*, or a noun filled with dramatic or even humorous resonance, like *leopard* or *scream* or *wiener*.

The second line is the longest, as the boomerang, blithe and vulnerable, spins out into the world, catching glints of sun and beads of dew. When you're writing it, there should be a thrill of danger in your heart, of teetering on the edge of some emotional cliff or failing grade.

The third line is slightly shorter but much less rebellious, breath released, as the boomerang follows a predictable arc towards home. And the final line, as short as the first but without its abandon, should feel as peaceful as taking the hand of someone you love—or pulling out the pin of a grenade.

Contributors' Notes:

Frances Payne Adler is the author of five books: two poetry collections: *The Making of a Matriot* (Red Hen Press, 2003) and *Raising the Tents* (Calyx Books, 1993); and three collaborative poetry-photography books and exhibitions with photographer Kira Carrillo Corser: *When The Bough Breaks: Pregnancy and The Legacy of Addiction* (NewSage Press, 1993), *Struggle To Be Borne* (San Diego State University Press, 1987), and *Home Street Home* (Red Cross, 1984), that have traveled the country, showing in galleries and state capitol buildings. Their most recent exhibition, "A Matriot's Dream: Health Care For All," showed on Capitol Hill in Washington, D.C. It is on permanent loan to the Universal Health Care Action Network and can be viewed on-line at www.matriot.org. Most recently, Adler co-edited *Fire and Ink: An Anthology of Social Action Writing* (University of Arizona Press, 2009) with poet Diana Garcia and fiction writer Debra Busman. Her awards include a California State Senate Award for Artistic and Social Collaboration, a National Endowment for the Arts Regional Award, and the New Millennium Obama Award. Adler is a professor and founder of the Creative Writing and Social Action Program at California State University Monterey Bay.

Erinn Batykefer was born in Pittsburgh, Pennsylvania during one of the coldest Januaries on record and grew up dividing her time between Northland Public Library, where she worked as a page (read: hid in the stacks and read voraciously, ears pricked for the sound of footsteps and heart pounding at the very thought of getting caught), and the Allegheny River, where she learned to row. Erinn attended the University of Delaware where she studied painting and ceramics before switching majors to concentrate on writing. In 2004, she graduated summa cum laude with a BA in English/Creative Writing and Art History and went on to earn her MFA in poetry from the University of Wisconsin-Madison, where she was a Martha Meier Renk Distinguished Poetry Fellow.

Elizabeth Bradfield grew up in the Pacific Northwest and has since called Cape Cod and Alaska home. She is the author of two poetry collections, *Interpretive Work* (2008) and *Approaching Ice* (2010). *The Atlantic Monthly*, *Poetry*, and *Field* have published her poems, as well as the anthologies *Best New Poets 2006* and *Joyful Noise: An Anthology of American Spiritual Poetry*. Bradfield's awards include several Pushcart Prize nominations, a scholarship at the Bread Loaf Writer's Conference, and a Wallace Stegner Fellowship. She holds an MFA from the University of Alaska Anchorage and is founder and editor of *Broadsided*. When not writing, she works as a web designer and naturalist.

Gaylord Brewer's most recent books are the poetry collection *The Martini Diet* (Dream Horse Press, 2008; winner of the 2006 Orphic Prize) and the comic novella *Octavius the 1st* (Red Hen Press, 2008). Red Hen will publish *Give Over, Graymalkin*, his eighth book of poetry, in 2011. His critical works include *David Mamet and Film* (McFarland, 1993) and *Charles Bukowski* (Macmillan, 1997). He has published 700+ poems in journals and anthologies, such as *Best American Poetry* and *The Bedford Introduction to Literature*, and his plays have been staged in Chicago, Columbus, Nashville, New York, and Valdez, Alaska. Among his recent residencies were Can Serrat and the Fundación Valparaíso, both in Spain. Brewer teaches at Middle Tennessee State University, where he founded and edits the journal *Poems & Plays*, and in the low-residency MFA program at Murray State University. He's also taught in Russia, Kenya, and the Czech Republic.

Bart Edelman was born in Paterson, New Jersey in 1951 and spent his childhood in Teaneck. He received his undergraduate and graduate degrees from Hofstra University. He is currently a professor of English at Glendale College, where he edits *Eclipse, A Literary Journal*. He was awarded grants and fellowships from the United States Department of Education, the University of Southern California, and the L.B.J. School of Public Affairs at the University of Texas at Austin, conducting literary research in India, Egypt, Nigeria, and Poland. His poetry has appeared in newspapers and journals, as well as textbooks and anthologies, published by City Lights Books, Etruscan Press, Harcourt Brace, McGraw-Hill, Prentice Hall, Simon & Schuster, Thomson/Heinle, and the

University of Iowa Press. He teaches poetry workshops across the United States and was Poet-in-Residence at Monroe College of the State University of New York. Collections of his work include *Crossing the Hackensack* (1993), *Under Damaris' Dress* (1996), *The Alphabet of Love* (1999), *The Gentle Man* (2001), and *The Last Mojito* (2005). He lives in Pasadena, California.

Ed Falco is a novelist, short story writer, playwright, and author of literary and experimental short fictions and new media compositions. His books include the short story collections *Acid* and *Burning Man* and the novels *Saint John of the Five Boroughs* and *Wolf Point*. He is the recipient of an NEA Fellowship in Fiction, the Robert Warren Penn Prize in Poetry, and a Virginia Commission for the Arts fellowship in playwriting. Ed lives in Blacksburg, Virginia, where he is the director of the MFA Program in Creative Writing at Virginia Tech.

Kate Gale, 2005–2006 President of PEN USA and president of American Composers Forum/LA, writes poetry, novels, and librettos. Kate Gale has taken the road less travelled. Rather than become a writer with a tenure-track job, she became a writer with two small children. Rather than mourn the lack of literary community in her adopted city of Los Angeles, she decided to create one in the form of Red Hen Press, Los Angeles' literary jewel, *The Los Angeles Review*, a literary magazine, the Ruskin Art Club Poetry Series, the Geffen reading series, and a Writers in the Schools program for underserved communities. At forty, she completed her PhD in literature from Claremont Graduate University, ran her first marathon, and climbed Mt. Whitney, the tallest mountain in the lower forty-eight. Kate Gale's *Rio de Sangre,* an opera with Don Davis, was performed in part at Disney Hall, November of 2005, and her opera *Paradises Lost* was performed in part at the New York City Opera in May of 2006. With publications including five collections of poetry, a novel, and a children's book, for Kate, the journey has just begun. She has poetry, a novella, and new librettos in process, a literary community to energize, and new writers to mentor. May all the ink-stained wenches be so lucky.

DeWitt Henry received a Massachusetts Commonwealth Award in 1992 for directing *Ploughshares*, one of the leading literary magazines in the country. Henry's novel, *The Marriage of Anna Maye Potts*, won the inaugural Peter Taylor Prize. Jack Smith wrote: "The novel evokes in the reader a sense for the power of the heart and will to transform one's self—and to make claims on what's rightfully one's own." The same can be said for *Safe Suicide* (Red Hen Press, 2008). Henry is a professor at Emerson College in Boston. He has also edited five anthologies, including *Sorrows Company: Writers on Loss and Grief* and (with James Alan McPherson) *Fathering Daughters: Reflections by Men*. His childhood memoir, *Sweet Dreams*, will appear from Hidden River Press in 2011.

Charles Hood is a Fulbright scholar in ethnopoetics and a contributing editor to the *Los Angeles Review*. Hood is also a research associate at the Getty, the Huntington, the Natural History Museum in London, and the Center for Land Use Interpretation, with whom he also has been Artist in Residence. Previous books include *Red Sky, Red Water*, a book about John Wesley Powell and the Colorado River, a rain forest book called *Xopilote Cantos*, and *The Half-Life of Salt: Voices from the* Enola Gay.

Douglas Kearney's first full-length collection of poems, *Fear, Some*, was published in 2006 by Red Hen Press. His second manuscript, *The Black Automaton*, was chosen by Catherine Wagner for the National Poetry Series and published by Fence Books in 2009. In 2008, he was honored with a Whiting Writers Award. Also a librettist, he has collaborated with the composer Anne LeBaron on the opera *Sucktion*, which received a MAP Fund grant and premiered at the New Original Works Festival in Los Angeles in 2008, and on *Mordake* with composer Erling Wold, which premiered in 2008 at the San Francisco International Arts Festival. An Idyllwild and Cave Canem fellow, Kearney has performed his poetry at the Public Theatre, Orpheum, and the World Stage. His poems have appeared in journals such as *Callaloo*, *jubilat*, *nocturnes*, *Ninth Letter*, *Washington Square*, and *Gulf Coast*. Kearney teaches at California Institute of the Arts.

Ron Koertge grew up in an old mining town in Illinois, on the banks of the Mississippi River. He has lived in California for many years and has been on the faculty of

Pasadena City College for more than 35 years. He also teaches in the MFA Writing for Children and Young Adults Program at Hamline University. He is the author of several acclaimed novels, including *The Arizona Kid*, *Stoner & Spaz*, and *Strays*, all of which were ALA Best Books for Young Adults.

Lisa C. Krueger has published two books of poetry and a series of interactive journals related to psychology and creativity. Her poetry has appeared in numerous publications. As a clinical psychologist, she maintains a private therapy practice focused on women's issues, writing therapy, and the role of creativity in wellness. She lives in Pasadena.

Sebastian Matthews is the author of the memoir *In My Father's Footsteps* and co-editor, with Stanley Plumly, of *Search Party: Collected Poems of William Matthews*. Matthews lives with his wife and son in Asheville, North Carolina, where he teaches part-time at Warren Wilson College and the Great Smokies Writing Program and edits *Rivendell*, a place-based literary journal.

Deena Metzger is a novelist, poet, essayist, and storyteller seeking to map the imaginal realms. She is an explorer of the deeper meaning and manifestations of Story. She works as a peace builder, healer, and medicine woman. Deena is the author of many works, including *Ruin and Beauty: New and Selected Poems*, *Grief Into Vision: A Council*, *Entering the Ghost River: Meditations on the Theory and Practice of Healing*, *Tree: Essays and Pieces*, *Writing For Your Life: A Guide and Companion to the Inner Worlds*, and the novels *The Other Hand*, *Doors*, and *What Dinah Thought*. She co-edited *Intimate Nature: The Bond Between Women and Animals*. She is known for her exuberant "Warrior" poster that illustrates the triumph over breast cancer.

Cecile Rossant, an experimental writer, combines poetry and prose in *About Face* in order to reveal how poetic form influences narrative form. A student of biology, painting, sculpture, and architecture, Cecile moved from New York to Tokyo, and finally Berlin, where she has worked as an architect. A twenty-first century Renaissance woman, Rossant is like the great artists and thinkers of that era, as her work is profoundly humanistic. In "Horizontal Drainage," for instance, Rossant explores the question of whether it is possible for a person to reject his or her historically-defined past for a new identity, bringing to the reader's mind an awareness of the paradox of humanistic study, in which one must alienate oneself from humanity in order to study it. Rossant is also the author of the novel *Tokyo Bay Traffic* (Red Hen Press, 2008) and the children's book *Underground New York* (Cornelsen, 2009).

Miriam Sagan was born in Manhattan, New York. She holds a BA with honors from Harvard University and an MA in Creative Writing from Boston University. She lived on the coastal extremes of San Francisco and Martha's Vineyard before settling in Santa Fe in 1984. Sagan is the recipient of a grant from The Barbara Deming Foundation/ Money for Women.

Greg Sanders's book of short stories, *Motel Girl*, was published by Red Hen Press in 2008. His writing has also appeared in numerous magazines and journals, including *The Los Angeles Review, Essays & Fictions,* and *The Warwick Review*. Greg lives in New York City.

Eva Saulitis, a poet, essayist, and biologist, received an MS in Marine Biology and an MFA in Creative Writing from the University of Alaska Fairbanks. She has published poems and essays in numerous journals and anthologies including *Crazyhorse, Prairie Schooner, Cimarron Review, Northwest Review,* and others. She has received fellowships from the Alaska State Council on the Arts, the Island Institute, the Rasmuson Foundation, and, in March 2007, was awarded a residency at Ventspils House, a center for writing and translation in Latvia. For the past 20 years, she has spent the summers studying killer and humpback whales in Prince William Sound, Alaska. She teaches creative writing and English at the University of Alaska and through the Artist in the Schools program in Homer, Alaska.

Shelley Savren, author of *The Common Fire* (Red Hen Press, 2004), holds an MFA from Antioch University Los Angeles. She is the recipient of nine California Arts

Council Artist in Residence grants, two National Endowment for the Arts regional grants, and five artist fellowships from the City of Ventura. She also received first place in the 1994 John David Johnson Memorial Poetry Award and a nomination for a Pushcart Prize. She has taught poetry writing workshops at a maximum security men's prison, juvenile detention centers, a homeless shelter, a school for emotionally disturbed adolescents, a women's center, and numerous other facilities and at every grade level through the California Poets in the Schools. She lives in Ventura, California and is a full-time English professor at Oxnard College. The Midwest Book Review writes: "*The Common Fire* showcases this remarkable talent and will aptly serve to introduce a whole new audience of readers to a storytelling poetry." Marge Piercy writes: "Shelley Savren's poems in *The Common Fire* are warm and direct, full of the stuff of daily life, family life, joy and pleasure and grief and pain we can all identify with in poems that carry a strong emotional weight." Li-Young Lee writes: "These are poems of earnest storytelling and fond description. Nostalgia for gone worlds and affection for the evanescing present are the subjects and inspirations for this volume. A pleasure to read."

Steven Schutzman is a playwright and fiction writer, the author of nine published books and of numerous plays and stories in literary journals including *The Pushcart Prize*, *TriQuarterly*, *Alaska Quarterly Review*, *Painted Bride Quarterly*, *Third Coast*, *Scene 4*, *Gargoyle*, *Night Train*, and the new anthology *The Art of the One Act*. More than thirty different plays of his have been produced at such theatres as New Jersey Repertory, Cleveland Public, Baltimore Theatre Project, Rochester Repertory, Circus Theatricals, and Revolution Theatre in Chicago among many others. He is a five-time recipient of Maryland State Arts Council Individual Artist Grant Awards and a three-time top tier finalist for the Eugene O'Neill Center National Playwrights Conference. His one-act "Tree Man" won first prize in the First Stage L.A. One-Act Contest (2004). His full-length play *A Question of Water* was chosen as the unanimous, inaugural selection for the Across the Generations New Jewish Play Festival, 2010.

Julie Shigekuni is the author of three novels: *A Bridge Between Us* (Anchor/Doubleday, 1995), *Invisible Gardens* (St. Martin's Press, 2003), and *Unending Nora* (Red Hen

Press, 2008). Her fiction has been translated into German, Swedish, Danish, and Norwegian. Shigekuni was a finalist for the Barnes & Noble Discover Great New Writers Award and the recipient of the PEN Oakland Josephine Miles Award for Excellence in Literature. She has received a Henfield Award and an American Japanese Literary Award for her writing. Shigekuni received her BA from CUNY Hunter College and her MFA from Sarah Lawrence College. She is currently at work on a collection of inter-connected short stories and a 60-minute video documentary, *Manju Mammas & the An-Pan Brigade*, for which she has received funding from the California Council for the Humanities and the Skirball Foundation and sponsorship from Visual Communications, an all-Asian media network. She teaches fiction and Asian American Literature at the University of New Mexico and lives in Corrales, New Mexico, with her husband and three young daughters.

Peggy Shumaker grew up in Tucson, Arizona, in the Sonoran desert. She has lived much of her adult life in Interior Alaska, where she taught at University of Alaska Fairbanks. Her poems spring from hidden sources—rivers beneath arroyos, inside glaciers, under the ocean. Her books of poems include *Blaze, Underground Rivers*, and *Gnawed Bones*. Her lyrical memoir *Just Breathe Normally* deals with putting life back together after major injuries from a bicycle wreck. Please visit her website at www.peggyshumaker.com.

Maurya Simon is the author of *The Enchanted Room* and *Days of Awe* (Copper Canyon Press, 1986, 1989), *Speaking in Tongues* (Gibbs Smith, 1990), *The Golden Labyrinth* (University of Missouri Press, 1995), *A Brief History of Punctuation* (Sutton Hoo Press, 2002), and *Weavers*, a collaborative work with Los Angeles artist Baila Goldenthal (Blackbird Press, 2003). Simon is the recipient of a 2002 Visiting Artist Fellowship from the American Academy in Rome, a 1999–2000 NEA Fellowship in poetry, a University Award from the Academy of American Poets, the Celia B. Wagner and Lucille Medwick Memorial Awards from the Poetry Society of America, and a Fulbright-Indo-American Fellowship. Simon has been a fellow at Hawthornden Castle in Edinburgh, Scotland and at the Baltic Centre for Writers and Translators in Visby, Sweden, as well as a lecturer at Lund University in Sweden. Her poems have appeared in *The New Yorker*, *Poetry*, *TriQuarterly*, *The Kenyon Review*, *The Georgia Review*, *The Gettysburg Review*, *Grand Street*, *Agni*, *Ploughshares*, *Shenandoah*, *The Los Angeles Times Book Review*, *The New England Review*, and in more than twenty-five anthologies. She teaches in the Creative Writing Department at the University of California, Riverside and lives in the Angeles National Forest of the San Gabriel Mountains in Southern California.

Lisa Russ Spaar, Professor of English and Creative Writing at the University of Virginia, is the author of *Satin Cash: Poems* (Persea Books, 2008), *Blue Venus: Poems* (Persea Books, 2004), and *Glass Town: Poems* (Red Hen Press, 1999), for which she received a Rona Jaffe Award for Emerging Women Writers in 2000, as well as two chapbooks. She is editor of *Acquainted With the Night: Insomnia Poems* (Columbia UP, 1999) and *All That Mighty Heart: London Poems* (University of Virginia Press, 2008). Her work is often anthologized and has appeared in many literary quarterlies and journals. Her work appears in *Best American Poetry 2008*, and her awards include a 2009/2010 Guggenheim Fellowship for Poetry, a University of Virginia All-University Teaching Award, and a 2010 Outstanding Faculty Award from the State Council of Higher Education for Virginia.

Charles Harper Webb's books of poetry include *Reading the Water*, *Liver*, *Tulip Farms and Leper Colonies*, *Hot Popsicles*, *Amplified Dog*, and *Stand Up Poetry: An Expanded Anthology*, which he edited. *Shadow Ball: New and Selected Poems* was published in 2009 by the University of Pittsburgh Press. Among Webb's awards are the Morse Poetry Prize, the Kate Tufts Discovery Award, the Felix Pollock Prize, the Benjamin Saltman Prize, a Whiting Writer's Award, and a Guggenheim Fellowship. A former rock singer/guitarist and psychotherapist, he directs the MFA Program at California State University, Long Beach.

Sholeh Wolpé is the author of *Rooftops of Tehran*, *The Scar Saloon*, and *Sin: Selected Poems of Forugh Farrokhzad*, for which she was awarded the Lois Roth Translation Prize in 2010 by the American Institute of Iranian Studies. Sholeh is the associate editor of *Tablet & Pen: Literary Landscapes from the Modern Middle East* (Norton), the guest editor of *Atlanta Review* (2010 Iran issue), and the poetry editor of the *Levantine Review*, an online journal about the Middle East. Her poems, translations, essays, and reviews have appeared in scores of literary journals, periodicals, and anthologies worldwide and have been translated into several languages. Sholeh was born in Iran and presently lives in Los Angeles.

DEAD MEN TALKING

WORKS BY DEAD PEOPLE
edited by
Robert Kane

Cover Art by Gustave Doré
Works selected by William Goldstein, Kate Holguin, Chris Konish, and Robert Kane

Contents

ELIZABETH BROWNING
    Amy's Cruelty   155

UNKNOWN
    The Viking Terror   159

SAROJINI NAIDU
    The Queen's Rival   160

UNKNOWN
    The Poem that Is in the Hall of the Tomb . . .   164

MICHELANGELO BUONARROTI
    On the Painting of the Sistine Chapel   167

ALICE DUNBAR NELSON
    Amid the Roses   168

UNKNOWN
    The Raven Who Wanted a Wife   169

EDGAR ALLAN POE
    The Masque of the Red Death   171

OSCAR WILDE
    The Canterville Ghost: Chapter 5   179

JAMES ELROY FLECKER
    Hassan   182

Contributors' Epitaphs   191

Elizabeth Browning

Amy's Cruelty

I

Fair Amy of the terraced house,
    Assist me to discover
Why you who would not hurt a mouse
    Can torture so your lover.

II

You give your coffee to the cat,
    You stroke the dog for coming,
And all your face grows kinder at
    The little brown bee's humming.

III

But when *he* haunts your door ... the town
    Marks coming and marks going ...
You seem to have stitched your eyelids down
    To that long piece of sewing!

IV

You never give a look, not you,
    Nor drop him a "Good morning,"
To keep his long day warm and blue,
    So fretted by your scorning.

V

She shook her head—"The mouse and bee
    For crumb or flower will linger:
The dog is happy at my knee,
    The cat purrs at my finger.

VI

"But *he* . . . to *him*, the least thing given
    Means great things at a distance;
He wants my world, my sun, my heaven,
    Soul, body, whole existence.

VII

"They say love gives as well as takes;
    But I'm a simple maiden,—
My mother's first smile when she wakes
    I still have smiled and prayed in.

VIII

"I only know my mother's love
    Which gives all and asks nothing;
And this new loving sets the groove
    Too much the way of loathing.

IX

"Unless he gives me all in change,
   I forfeit all things by him:
The risk is terrible and strange—
   I tremble, doubt, . . . deny him.

X

"He's sweetest friend or hardest foe,
   Best angel or worst devil;
I either hate or . . . love him so,
   I can't be merely civil!

XI

"You trust a woman who puts forth
   Her blossoms thick as summer's?
You think she dreams what love is worth,
   Who casts it to new-comers?

XII

"Such love's a cowslip-ball to fling,
   A moment's pretty pastime;
I give . . . all me, if anything,
   The first time and the last time.

XIII
"Dear neighbour of the trellised house,
    A man should murmur never,
Though treated worse than dog and mouse,
    Till doated on for ever!"

Unknown

The Viking Terror

Bitter is the wind to-night,
It tosses the ocean's white hair:
To-night I fear not the fierce warriors of Norway
Coursing on the Irish Sea.

Translated by Kuno Meyer

Sarojini Naidu

The Queen's Rival

QUEEN Gulnaar sat on her ivory bed,
Around her countless treasures were spread;

Her chamber walls were richly inlaid
With agate, porphory, onyx and jade;

The tissues that veiled her delicate breast,
Glowed with the hues of a lapwing's crest;

But still she gazed in her mirror and sighed
"O King, my heart is unsatisfied."

King Feroz bent from his ebony seat:
"Is thy least desire unfulfilled, O Sweet?

"Let thy mouth speak and my life be spent
To clear the sky of thy discontent."

"I tire of my beauty, I tire of this
Empty splendour and shadowless bliss;

"With none to envy and none gainsay,
No savour or salt hath my dream or day."

Queen Gulnaar sighed like a murmuring rose:
"Give me a rival, O King Feroz."

II

King Feroz spoke to his Chief Vizier:
"Lo! ere to-morrow's dawn be here,

"Send forth my messengers over the sea,
To seek seven beautiful brides for me;

"Radiant of feature and regal of mien,
Seven handmaids meet for the Persian Queen."

Seven new moon tides at the Vesper call,
King Feroz led to Queen Gulnaar's hall

A young queen eyed like the morning star:
"I bring thee a rival, O Queen Gulnaar."

But still she gazed in her mirror and sighed:
"O King, my heart is unsatisfied."

Seven queens shone round her ivory bed,
Like seven soft gems on a silken thread,

Like seven fair lamps in a royal tower,
Like seven bright petals of Beauty's flower

Queen Gulnaar sighed like a murmuring rose
"Where is my rival, O King Feroz?"

III

When spring winds wakened the mountain floods,
And kindled the flame of the tulip buds,
When bees grew loud and the days grew long,
And the peach groves thrilled to the oriole's song,

Queen Gulnaar sat on her ivory bed,
Decking with jewels her exquisite head;

And still she gazed in her mirror and sighed:
"O King, my heart is unsatisfied."

Queen Gulnaar's daughter two spring times old,
In blue robes bordered with tassels of gold,

Ran to her knee like a wildwood fay,
And plucked from her hand the mirror away.

Quickly she set on her own light curls
Her mother's fillet with fringes of pearls;

Quickly she turned with a child's caprice
And pressed on the mirror a swift, glad kiss.

Queen Gulnaar laughed like a tremulous rose:
"Here is my rival, O King Feroz."

Unknown

> The Poem that Is in the Hall of the Tomb of
> [The King of the South, the King of the North],
> Antuf, Whose Word is Truth, [And is Cut]
> In Front of the Harper

O good prince, it is a decree,
And what hath been ordained thereby is well,
That the bodies of men shall pass away and disappear,
Whilst others remain.

Since the time of the oldest ancestors,
The gods who lived in olden time,
Who lie at rest in their sepulchres,
The Masters and also the Shining Ones,
Who have been buried in their splendid tombs,
Who have built sacrificial halls in their tombs,
Their place is no more.
Consider what hath become of them!

I have heard the words of Imhetep, and Herutataf
Which are treasured above everything because they uttered them.
Consider what hath become of their tombs!
Their walls have been thrown down;
Their places are no more;
They are just as if they had never existed.

Not one [of them] cometh from where they are.
Who can describe to us their form (or, condition),
Who can describe to us their surroundings,

Who can give comfort to our hearts,
And can act as our guide
To the place whereunto they have departed?

Give comfort to thy heart,
And let thy heart forget these things;
What is best for thee to do is
To follow thy heart's desire as long as thou livest.

Anoint thy head with scented unguents.
Let thine apparel be of byssus
Dipped in costly [perfumes],
In the veritable products (?) of the gods.

Enjoy thyself more than thou hast ever done before,
And let not thy heart pine for lack of pleasure.

Pursue thy heart's desire and thine own happiness.
Order thy surroundings on earth in such a way
That they may minister to the desire of thy heart;
[For] at length that day of lamentation shall come,
Wherein he whose heart is still shall not hear the lamentation.
Never shall cries of grief cause
To beat [again] the heart of a man who is in the grave.

Therefore occupy thyself with thy pleasure daily,
And never cease to enjoy thyself.

Behold, a man is not permitted
To carry his possessions away with him.
Behold, there never was any one who, having departed,
Was able to come back again.

Translated by E.A. Wallis Budge

Michelangelo Buonarroti

On the Painting of the Sistine Chapel
To Giovanni da Pistoja

I've grown a goitre by dwelling in this den—
    As cats from stagnant streams in Lombardy,
    Or in what other land they hap to be—
    Which drives the belly close beneath the chin:
My beard turns up to heaven; my nape falls in,
    Fixed on my spine: my breast-bone visibly
    Grows like a harp: a rich embroidery
    Bedews my face from brush-drops thick and thin.
My loins into my paunch like levers grind:
    My buttock like a crupper bears my weight;
    My feet unguided wander to and fro;
In front my skin grows loose and long; behind,
    By bending it becomes more taut and strait;
    Crosswise I strain me like a Syrian bow:
        Whence false and quaint, I know,
    Must be the fruit of squinting brain and eye;
    For ill can aim the gun that bends awry.
        Come then, Giovanni, try
    To succour my dead pictures and my fame;
    Since foul I fare and painting is my shame.

Alice Dunbar Nelson

Amid the Roses

There is tropical warmth and languorous life
    Where the roses lie
    In a tempting drift
Of pink and red and golden light
Untouched as yet by the pruning knife.
And the still, warm life of the roses fair
    That whisper "Come,"
    With promises
Of sweet caresses, close and pure
Has a thorny whiff in the perfumed air.
There are thorns and love in the roses' bed,
    And Satan too
    Must linger there;
So Satan's wiles and the conscience stings,
Must now abide—the roses are *dead*.

Unknown

The Raven Who Wanted a Wife

A little sparrow was mourning for her husband who was lost. She was very fond of him, for he caught worms for her.

As she sat there weeping, a raven came up to her and asked:

"Why are you weeping?"

"I am weeping for my husband, who is lost; I was fond of him, because he caught worms for me," said the sparrow.

"It is not fitting for one to weep who can hop over high blades of grass," said the raven. "Take me for a husband; I have a fine high forehead, broad temples, a long beard and a big beak; you shall sleep under my wings, and I will give you lovely offal to eat."

"I will not take you for a husband, for you have a high forehead, broad temples, a long beard and a big beak, and will give me offal to eat."

So the raven flew away—flew off to seek a wife among the wild geese. And he was so lovesick that he could not sleep.

When he came to the wild geese, they were about to fly away to other lands.

Said the raven to two of the geese:

"Seeing that a miserable sparrow has refused me, I will have you."

"We are just getting ready to fly away," said the geese.

"I will go too," said the raven.

"But consider this: that none can go with us who cannot swim or rest upon the surface of the water. For there are no icebergs along the way we go."

"It is nothing; I will sail through the air," said the raven.

And the wild geese flew away, and the raven with them. But very soon he felt himself sinking from weariness and lack of sleep.

"Something to rest on!" cried the raven, gasping. "Sit you down side by side." And his two wives sat down together on the water, while their comrades flew on.

The raven sat down on them and fell asleep. But when his wives saw the other geese flying farther and farther away, they dropped that raven into the sea and flew off after them.

"Something to rest on!" gasped the raven, as it fell into the water. And at last it went to the bottom and was drowned.

And after a while, it broke up into little pieces, and its soul was turned into little "sea ravens."

Translated by W. Worster

Edgar Allan Poe

The Masque of the Red Death

The "Red Death" had long devastated the country. No pestilence had ever been so fatal, or so hideous. Blood was its Avatar and its seal—the redness and the horror of blood. There were sharp pains, and sudden dizziness, and then profuse bleeding at the pores, with dissolution. The scarlet stains upon the body and especially upon the face of the victim, were the pest ban which shut him out from the aid and from the sympathy of his fellow-men. And the whole seizure, progress and termination of the disease, were the incidents of half an hour.

But the Prince Prospero was happy and dauntless and sagacious. When his dominions were half depopulated, he summoned to his presence a thousand hale and light-hearted friends from among the knights and dames of his court, and with these retired to the deep seclusion of one of his castellated abbeys. This was an extensive and magnificent structure, the creation of the prince's own eccentric yet august taste. A strong and lofty wall girdled it in. This wall had gates of iron. The courtiers, having entered, brought furnaces and massy hammers and welded the bolts. They resolved to leave means neither of ingress nor egress to the sudden impulses of despair or of frenzy from within. The abbey was amply provisioned. With such precautions the courtiers might bid defiance to contagion. The external world could take care of itself. In the meantime it was folly to grieve, or to think. The prince had provided all the appliances of pleasure. There were buffoons, there were improvisatori, there were ballet-dancers, there were musicians, there was Beauty, there was wine. All these and security were within. Without was the "Red Death".

It was towards the close of the fifth or sixth month of his seclusion, and while the pestilence raged most furiously abroad, that the Prince Prospero entertained his thousand friends at a masked ball of the most unusual magnificence.

It was a voluptuous scene, that masquerade. But first let me tell of the rooms in which it was held. These were seven—an imperial suite. In many palaces, however, such suites form a long and straight vista, while the folding doors slide back nearly to the walls on either hand, so that the view of the whole extent is scarcely impeded. Here the case was very different, as might have been expected from the duke's love of the *bizarre*. The apartments were so irregularly disposed that the vision embraced but little more than one at a time. There was a sharp turn at every twenty or thirty yards, and at each turn a novel effect. To the right and left, in the middle of each wall, a tall and narrow Gothic window looked out upon a closed corridor which pursued the windings of the suite. These windows were of stained glass whose colour varied in accordance with the prevailing hue of the decorations of the chamber into which it opened. That at the eastern extremity was hung, for example in blue—and vividly blue were its windows. The second chamber was purple in its ornaments and tapestries, and here the panes were purple. The third was green throughout, and so were the casements. The fourth was furnished and lighted with orange—the fifth with white—the sixth with violet. The seventh apartment was closely shrouded in black velvet tapestries that hung all over the ceiling and down the walls, falling in heavy folds upon a carpet of the same material and hue. But in this chamber only, the colour of the windows failed to correspond with the decorations. The panes here were scarlet—a deep blood colour. Now in no one of the seven apartments was there any lamp or candelabrum, amid the profusion of golden ornaments that lay scattered to and fro or depended from the roof. There was no light of any kind emanating from lamp or candle within the suite of chambers. But in the corridors that followed the suite, there stood, opposite to each window, a heavy tripod, bearing a brazier of fire, that projected its rays through the tinted glass and so glaringly illumined the room. And thus were produced a multitude of gaudy and fantastic appearances. But in the western or black chamber the effect of the fire-light that streamed upon the dark hangings through the blood-tinted panes, was ghastly in the extreme, and produced so wild a look upon the countenances of those who entered, that there were few of the company bold enough to set foot within its precincts at all.

It was in this apartment, also, that there stood against the western wall, a gigantic clock of ebony. Its pendulum swung to and fro with a dull, heavy, monotonous clang; and when the minute-hand made the circuit of the face, and the hour was to be stricken, there came from the brazen lungs of the clock a sound which was clear and loud and deep and exceedingly musical, but of so peculiar a note and emphasis that, at each lapse of an hour, the musicians of the orchestra were constrained to pause, momentarily, in their performance, to harken to the sound; and thus the waltzers perforce ceased their evolutions; and there was a brief disconcert of the whole gay company; and, while the chimes of the clock yet rang, it was observed that the giddiest grew pale, and the more aged and sedate passed their hands over their brows as if in confused revery or meditation. But when the echoes had fully ceased, a light laughter at once pervaded the assembly; the musicians looked at each other and smiled as if at their own nervousness and folly, and made whispering vows, each to the other, that the next chiming of the clock should produce in them no similar emotion; and then, after the lapse of sixty minutes, (which embrace three thousand and six hundred seconds of the Time that flies,) there came yet another chiming of the clock, and then were the same disconcert and tremulousness and meditation as before.

But, in spite of these things, it was a gay and magnificent revel. The tastes of the duke were peculiar. He had a fine eye for colours and effects. He disregarded the *decora* of mere fashion. His plans were bold and fiery, and his conceptions glowed with barbaric lustre. There are some who would have thought him mad. His followers felt that he was not. It was necessary to hear and see and touch him to be *sure* that he was not.

He had directed, in great part, the movable embellishments of the seven chambers, upon occasion of this great *fête*; and it was his own guiding taste which had given character to the masqueraders. Be sure they were grotesque. There were much glare and glitter and piquancy and phantasm—much of what has been since seen in "Hernani". There were arabesque figures with unsuited limbs and appointments. There were delirious fancies such as the madman fashions. There were much of the beautiful, much of the wanton, much of the *bizarre*, something of the terrible, and not a little of that which might have excited disgust. To and fro in the seven chambers there stalked, in fact, a multitude of dreams. And these—the dreams—writhed in and about taking hue from the rooms, and causing the wild music of the orchestra to seem as the echo of their steps. And, anon, there strikes the ebony clock which stands in the hall of the velvet. And then, for a moment, all is still, and all is silent save the voice of the clock. The dreams are stiff-frozen as they stand. But the echoes of the chime die away—they have endured but an instant—and a light, half-subdued laughter floats after them as they depart. And now again the music swells, and the dreams live, and writhe to and fro more merrily than ever, taking hue from the many tinted windows through which stream the rays from the tripods. But to the chamber which lies most westwardly of the seven, there are now none of the maskers who venture; for the night is waning away; and there flows a ruddier light through the blood-coloured panes; and the blackness of the sable drapery appals; and to him whose foot falls upon the sable carpet, there comes from the near clock of ebony a muffled peal more solemnly emphatic than any which reaches *their* ears who indulged in the more remote gaieties of the other apartments.

But these other apartments were densely crowded, and in them beat feverishly the heart of life. And the revel went whirlingly on, until at length there commenced the sounding of midnight upon the clock. And then the music ceased, as I have told; and the evolutions of the waltzers were quieted; and there was an uneasy cessation of all things as before. But now there were twelve strokes to be sounded by the bell of the clock; and thus it happened, perhaps, that more of thought crept, with more of time, into the meditations of the thoughtful among those who revelled. And thus too, it happened, perhaps, that before the last echoes of the last chime had utterly sunk into silence, there were many individuals in the crowd who had found leisure to become aware of the presence of a masked figure which had arrested the attention of no single individual before. And the rumour of this new presence having spread itself whisperingly around, there arose at length from the whole company a buzz, or murmur, expressive of disapprobation and surprise—then, finally, of terror, of horror, and of disgust.

In an assembly of phantasms such as I have painted, it may well be supposed that no ordinary appearance could have excited such sensation. In truth the masquerade licence of the night was nearly unlimited; but the figure in question had out-Heroded Herod, and gone beyond the bounds of even the prince's indefinite decorum. There are chords in the hearts of the most reckless which cannot be touched without emotion. Even with the utterly lost, to whom life and death are equally jests, there are matters of which no jest can be made. The whole company, indeed, seemed now deeply to feel that in the costume and bearing of the stranger neither wit nor propriety existed. The figure was tall and gaunt, and shrouded from head to foot in the habiliments of the grave. The mask which concealed the visage was made so nearly to resemble the countenance of a stiffened corpse that the closest scrutiny must have had difficulty in detecting the cheat. And yet all this might have been endured, if not approved, by the mad revellers around. But the mummer had gone so far as to assume the type of the Red Death. His vesture was dabbled in *blood*—and his broad brow, with all the features of the face, was besprinkled with the scarlet horror.

When the eyes of the Prince Prospero fell upon this spectral image (which, with a slow and solemn movement, as if more fully to sustain its role, stalked to and fro among the waltzers) he was seen to be convulsed, in the first moment with a strong shudder either of terror or distaste; but, in the next, his brow reddened with rage.

"Who dares,"—he demanded hoarsely of the courtiers who stood near him— "who dares insult us with this blasphemous mockery? Seize him and unmask him—that we may know whom we have to hang, at sunrise, from the battlements!"

It was in the eastern or blue chamber in which stood the Prince Prospero as he uttered these words. They rang throughout the seven rooms loudly and clearly, for the prince was a bold and robust man, and the music had become hushed at the waving of his hand.

It was in the blue room where stood the prince, with a group of pale courtiers by his side. At first, as he spoke, there was a slight rushing movement of this group in the direction of the intruder, who at the moment was also near at hand, and now, with deliberate and stately step, made closer approach to the speaker. But from a certain nameless awe with which the mad assumptions of the mummer had inspired the whole party, there were found none who put forth hand to seize him; so that, unimpeded, he passed within a yard of the prince's person; and, while the vast assembly, as if with one impulse, shrank from the centres of the rooms to the walls, he made his way uninterruptedly, but with the same solemn and measured step which had distinguished him from the first, through the blue chamber to the purple—through the purple to the green—through the green to the orange—through this again to the white—and even thence to the violet, ere a decided movement had been made to arrest him. It was then, however, that the Prince Prospero, maddening with rage and the shame of his own momentary cowardice, rushed hurriedly through the six chambers, while none followed him on account of a deadly terror that had seized upon all. He bore aloft a drawn dagger, and had approached, in rapid impetuosity, to within three or four feet of the retreating figure, when the latter, having attained the extremity of the velvet apartment, turned suddenly and confronted his pursuer. There was a sharp cry—and the dagger dropped gleaming upon the sable carpet, upon which, instantly afterwards, fell prostrate in death the Prince Prospero. Then, summoning the wild courage of despair, a throng of the revellers at once threw themselves into the black apartment, and, seizing the mummer, whose tall figure stood erect and motionless within the shadow of the ebony clock, gasped in unutterable horror at finding the grave cerements and corpse-like mask, which they handled with so violent a rudeness, untenanted by any tangible form.

And now was acknowledged the presence of the Red Death. He had come like a thief in the night. And one by one dropped the revellers in the blood-bedewed halls of their revel, and died each in the despairing posture of his fall. And the life of the ebony clock went out with that of the last of the gay. And the flames of the tripods expired. And Darkness and Decay and the Red Death held illimitable dominion over all.

Oscar Wilde

The Canterville Ghost, Chapter 5

A few days after this, Virginia and her curly-haired cavalier went out riding on Brockley meadows, where she tore her habit so badly in getting through a hedge that, on their return home, she made up her mind to go up by the back staircase so as not to be seen. As she was running past the Tapestry Chamber, the door of which happened to be open, she fancied she saw some one inside, and thinking it was her mother's maid, who sometimes used to bring her work there, looked in to ask her to mend her habit. To her immense surprise, however, it was the Canterville Ghost himself! He was sitting by the window, watching the ruined gold of the yellowing trees fly through the air, and the red leaves dancing madly down the long avenue. His head was leaning on his hand, and his whole attitude was one of extreme depression. Indeed, so forlorn, and so much out of repair did he look, that little Virginia, whose first idea had been to run away and lock herself in her room, was filled with pity, and determined to try and comfort him. So light was her footfall, and so deep his melancholy, that he was not aware of her presence till she spoke to him.

"I am so sorry for you," she said, "but my brothers are going back to Eton tomorrow, and then, if you behave yourself, no one will annoy you."

"It is absurd asking me to behave myself," he answered, looking round in astonishment at the pretty little girl who had ventured to address him, "quite absurd. I must rattle my chains, and groan through keyholes, and walk about at night, if that is what you mean. It is my only reason for existing."

"It is no reason at all for existing, and you know you have been very wicked. Mrs. Umney told us, the first day we arrived here, that you had killed your wife."

"Well, I quite admit it," said the Ghost, petulantly, "but it was a purely family matter, and concerned no one else."

"It is very wrong to kill any one," said Virginia, who at times had a sweet puritan gravity, caught from some old New England ancestor.

"Oh, I hate the cheap severity of abstract ethics! My wife was very plain, never had my ruffs properly starched, and knew nothing about cookery. Why, there was a buck I had shot in Hogley Woods, a magnificent pricket, and do you know how she had it sent to table? However, it is no matter now, for it is all over, and I don't think it was very nice of her brothers to starve me to death, though I did kill her."

"Starve you to death? Oh, Mr. Ghost—I mean Sir Simon, are you hungry? I have a sandwich in my case. Would you like it?"

"No, thank you, I never eat anything now; but it is very kind of you, all the same, and you are much nicer than the rest of your horrid, rude, vulgar, dishonest family."

"Stop!" cried Virginia, stamping her foot, "it is you who are rude, and horrid, and vulgar, and as for dishonesty, you know you stole the paints out of my box to try and furbish up that ridiculous blood-stain in the library. First you took all my reds, including the vermilion, and I couldn't do any more sunsets, then you took the emerald-green and the chrome-yellow, and finally I had nothing left but indigo and Chinese white, and could only do moonlight scenes, which are always depressing to look at, and not at all easy to paint. I never told on you, though I was very much annoyed, and it was most ridiculous, the whole thing; for who ever heard of emerald-green blood?"

"Well, really," said the Ghost, rather meekly, "what was I to do? It is a very difficult thing to get real blood nowadays, and, as your brother began it all with his Paragon Detergent, I certainly saw no reason why I should not have your paints. As for colour, that is always a matter of taste: the Cantervilles have blue blood, for instance, the very bluest in England; but I know you Americans don't care for things of this kind."

"You know nothing about it, and the best thing you can do is to emigrate and improve your mind. My father will be only too happy to give you a free passage, and though there is a heavy duty on spirits of every kind, there will be no difficulty about the Custom House, as the officers are all Democrats. Once in New York, you are sure to be a great success. I know lots of people there who would give a hundred thousand dollars to have a grandfather, and much more than that to have a family ghost."

"I don't think I should like America."

"I suppose because we have no ruins and no curiosities," said Virginia, satirically.

"No ruins! no curiosities!" answered the Ghost; "you have your navy and your manners."

"Good evening; I will go and ask papa to get the twins an extra week's holiday."

"Please don't go, Miss Virginia," he cried; "I am so lonely and so unhappy, and I really don't know what to do. I want to go to sleep and I cannot."

"That's quite absurd! You have merely to go to bed and blow out the candle. It is very difficult sometimes to keep awake, especially at church, but there is no difficulty at all about sleeping. Why, even babies know how to do that, and they are not very clever."

"I have not slept for three hundred years," he said sadly, and Virginia's beautiful blue eyes opened in wonder; "for three hundred years I have not slept, and I am so tired."

Virginia grew quite grave, and her little lips trembled like rose-leaves. She came towards him, and kneeling down at his side, looked up into his old withered face.

"Poor, poor Ghost," she murmured; "have you no place where you can sleep?"

"Far away beyond the pine-woods," he answered, in a low dreamy voice, "there is a little garden. There the grass grows long and deep, there are the great white stars of the hemlock flower, there the nightingale sings all night long. All night long he sings, and the cold, crystal moon looks down, and the yew-tree spreads out its giant arms over the sleepers."

Virginia's eyes grew dim with tears, and she hid her face in her hands.

"You mean the Garden of Death," she whispered.

"Yes, Death. Death must be so beautiful. To lie in the soft brown earth, with the grasses waving above one's head, and listen to silence. To have no yesterday, and no to-morrow. To forget time, to forgive life, to be at peace. You can help me. You can open for me the portals of Death's house, for Love is always with you, and Love is stronger than Death is."

Virginia trembled, a cold shudder ran through her, and for a few moments there was silence. She felt as if she was in a terrible dream.

Then the Ghost spoke again, and his voice sounded like the sighing of the wind.

"Have you ever read the old prophecy on the library window?"

"Oh, often," cried the little girl, looking up; "I know it quite well. It is painted in curious black letters, and it is difficult to read. There are only six lines:

When a golden girl can win
Prayer from out the lips of sin,
When the barren almond bears,
And a little child gives away its tears,
Then shall all the house be still
And peace come to Canterville.

But I don't know what they mean."

"They mean," he said sadly, "that you must weep for me for my sins, because I have no tears, and pray with me for my soul, because I have no faith, and then, if you have always been sweet, and good, and gentle, the Angel of Death will have mercy on me. You will see fearful shapes in darkness, and wicked voices will whisper in your ear, but they will not harm you, for against the purity of a little child the powers of Hell cannot prevail."

Virginia made no answer, and the Ghost wrung his hands in wild despair as he looked down at her bowed golden head. Suddenly she stood up, very pale, and with a strange light in her eyes. "I am not afraid," she said firmly, "and I will ask the Angel to have mercy on you."

He rose from his seat with a faint cry of joy, and taking her hand bent over it with old-fashioned grace and kissed it. His fingers were as cold as ice, and his lips burned like fire, but Virginia did not falter, as he led her across the dusky room. On the faded green tapestry were broidered little huntsmen. They blew their tasselled horns and with their tiny hands waved to her to go back. "Go back! little Virginia," they cried, "go back!" but the Ghost clutched her hand more tightly, and she shut her eyes against them. Horrible animals with lizard tails, and goggle eyes, blinked at her from the carven chimney-piece, and murmured "Beware! little Virginia, beware! we may never see you again," but the Ghost glided on more swiftly, and Virginia did not listen. When they reached the end of the room he stopped, and muttered some words she could not understand. She opened her eyes, and saw the wall slowly fading away like a mist, and a great black cavern in front of her. A bitter cold wind swept round them, and she felt something pulling at her dress. "Quick, quick," cried the Ghost, "or it will be too late," and, in a moment, the wainscoting had closed behind them, and the Tapestry Chamber was empty.

James Elroy Flecker

Hassan: The Story of Hassan of Bagdad and How He Came to Make the Golden Journey to Samarkand

An Excerpt from Act V, Scene I

Characters:
HASSAN, a Confectioner
ISHAK, his Minstrel
THE FOUNTAIN GHOST
GHOST OF RAFI, King of the Beggars
GHOST HIDDEN IN THE TREES
GHOST OF PERVANEH
VOICES

> Scene: *The Garden of the Caliph's palace. A deep red afterglow illumines the back of the garden. The fountain runs red.*

HASSAN

The fountain—the fountain!

ISHAK

Oh! alas! it is pouring blood! Come away.

HASSAN

The Garden is alive!

ISHAK

Come away: it is haunted! Come away: come away! Follow the bells!

Exeunt in terror.

THE GHOST OF THE ARTIST OF THE FOUNTAIN *rises from the fountain itself in pale Byzantine robes.*

Fountain Ghost

The garden to the ghosts. Come forth, new brother and new sister. Come forth while enough of earth's heavy influence remains upon you—to speak and to be seen. Come forth, and those who are past shall dance with those who are to come.

Ghost of Rafi

(*With the voice of* RAFI, *the clothes of* RAFI, *the broken fetters of* RAFI, *but pale . . . as death*) We are here, O Shadow of the Fountain.

Fountain Ghost

Welcome, thou and thy white lady to these . . . haunts. Wander at will. I have scared away the sons of flesh.

Ghost of Rafi

How were they scared, those two?

Fountain Ghost

When the water turned from white to red their faces turned from red to white. They ran!

Ghost Hidden in the Trees

Ha! ha!

Ghost of Pervaneh

Tell us, O Man of the Fountain, what shall we do?

Fountain Ghost

Nothing: you are dead.

Ghost of Pervaneh

Shall we stay in this garden and be lovers still, and fly in the air and flit among the leaves?

Fountain Ghost

As long as you remember what you suffered, you will stay near the house where your blood was shed.

Ghost of Pervaneh

We will remember that ten thousand years.

Fountain Ghost

You have forgotten that you are a Spirit. The memories of the dead are thinner than their dreams.

Ghost of Pervaneh

But you stay here, by the fountain.

Fountain Ghost

I created the fountain: what have you created in the world?

Ghost of Pervaneh

Nothing but the story of our lives.

Fountain Ghost

That will not save you. You were spiritual even in life. I see it by the great shadows of your eyes. But I cared only for the earth. I loved the veins of the leaves, the shapes of crawling beasts, the puddle in the road, the feel of wood and stone. I knew the shapes of things so well that my sculpture was the best in the world. Therefore my spirit is still heavy with memories of earth and I stay in the world I love. Do I desire to see the back of the moon?

Ghost of Pervaneh

May not we stay also? May I not touch the shadow of his lips and hear the whisper of his love? Shall we be driven from here, O Man of the fountain?

Fountain Ghost

How do I know? Can I foresee?

Ghost of Pervaneh

Thou, too dost not foresee. But what of Paradise, what of Infinity—what of the stars, and what of us?

Fountain Ghost

I know no more than you.

Ghost of Pervaneh

Is the secret secret still, and this existence darker than the last?

Fountain Ghost

Didst thou hope for a revelation? Why should the dead be wiser than the living? The dead know only this—that it was better to be alive.

Ghost of Pervaneh

But we shall feel no more pain—Oh, no more pain, Rafi!

Fountain Ghost

But you will feel so cold.

Ghost of Pervaneh

With the fire of love within us?

Fountain Ghost

You will forget when the wind blows.

Ghost of Pervaneh

Forget! Rafi, Rafi, shall we forget, Rafi?

Ghost of Rafi

(*In a thin voice like an echo*) Forget . . . Rafi . . .

Fountain Ghost

You will forget, when the great wind blows you asunder and you are borne on it with ten million others like drops on a wave of air.

Ghost of Pervaneh

There is a faith in me that tells I shall not forget my lover though God forget the world. And where will the wind take us?

Fountain Ghost

What do I know, or they? I only know it rushes.

Ghost of Pervaneh

How do you know about the wind?

Fountain Ghost

Because it blows through the garden and drives the souls together.

GHOST OF PERVANEH
   What souls?

FOUNTAIN GHOST
   The souls of the unborn children who live in the flowers.

GHOST OF PERVANEH
   And how do you know about the passage of ten million souls?

FOUNTAIN GHOST
   They pass like a comet across the midnight skies.

GHOST OF PERVANEH
   Phantoms shall not make me fear. But what of Justice and Punishment and Reason and Desire? What of the Lover in the Garden of Peace?

FOUNTAIN GHOST
   Ask of the wind.

GHOST OF PERVANEH
   I shall be answered: I know that in the end I shall find the Lover in the Garden of Peace.

VOICES
   And what of Life?

GHOST OF PERVANEH
   Who asks, What of Life?

Fountain Ghost

The spirits of those who will soon be born.

Voices

We have left our flowers. We know we shall soon be born. What of Life, O dead?

Ghost of Pervaneh

(*With a great cry*) Why, Life . . . is sweet, my children!

The leaves of the trees begin to rustle.

Fountain Ghost

Listen to the tress.

Ghost of Pervaneh

Is it coming?

Fountain Ghost

It is the wind. I must go down into the earth.

The FOUNTAIN GHOST *vanishes.*

Ghost of Pervaneh

Ah, I am cold—I am cold—beloved!

Ghost of Rafi

(*Scarce visible and very faint*) Cold . . . cold.

Ghost of Pervaneh

Speak to me, speak to me, Rafi.

Ghost of Rafi

    Rafi—Rafi—who was Rafi?

Ghost of Pervaneh

    Speak to thy love—thy love—thy love.

Ghost of Rafi

    Cold . . . cold . . . cold.

The wind sweeps the GHOSTS *out of the garden . . .*

Contributors' Epitaphs:

Elizabeth Browning: "Love, strong as Death, shall conquer Death." Died June 29th, 1861.

E.A. Wallis Budge: "The man who has led a life free from lies and deceit shall live after death like a god." Died November 23rd, 1934.

Michelangelo Buonarotti: "... if Death hear my prayer and grant me grace, [m]y grief I shall forget, again made blest." Died February 18th, 1564.

Gustave Doré: "The present volume shows Gustave Doré as a master of the grotesque; and the Publishers appeal to the Public, to whom the volume is offered, confident in the expectation that the high estimate formed by those to whom these Sketches are already familiar, will be corroborated by the general verdict." Died January 23rd, 1883.

James Elroy Flecker: "I read my books all day, [b]ut death has taken all my books away." Died January 3rd, 1915.

Kuno Meyer: "Carry my blessing with thee to the West, [m]y heart is broken in my breast: Should sudden death overtake me, [i]t is for my great love of the Gael." Died October 11th, 1919.

Sarojini Naidu: "Lamp of my life, the lips of Death [h]ath blown thee out with their sudden breath." Died March 2nd, 1949.

Alice Dunbar Nelson: "A traveller who has always heard [t]hat on this journey he some day must go, [y]et shudders now, when at the fatal word [h]e starts upon the lonesome, dreary way. The past, a page of joy and woe,—the future, none can say."

Died September 18th, 1935.

Edgar Allan Poe: "I could not love except where Death [w]as mingling his with Beauty's breath—" Died October 7th, 1849.

Unknown: "Can you say whether the head was cut off before or after death?"

Oscar Wilde: "I am going to the House of Death. Death is the brother of Sleep, is he not?" Died November 30th, 1900.

W. Worster: "Better to be without day, if thus we may be without death." Died in 1929.

I thrust a torch through the remaining aperture and let it fall within. There came forth in reply only a jingling of the bells. My heart grew sick on account of the dampness of the catacombs. I hastened to make an end of my labour. I forced the last stone into its position; I plastered it up. Against the new masonry I re-erected the old rampart of bones. For the half of a century no mortal has disturbed them.

In pace requiescat!

—Edgar Allan Poe

www.ingramcontent.com/pod-product-compliance
Ingram Content Group UK Ltd.
Pitfield, Milton Keynes, MK11 3LW, UK
UKHW041919140426
5217IPUK00013B/228